HER FAITHFUL PROTECTOR

NIGHT STORM, BOOK SIX

CAITLYN O'LEARY

To all the people who need a second chance at love, I hope you'll find it.

SYNOPSIS

Will Nic Get His Second Chance At Love?

Navy SEAL, Nic Hale, is happy. Just ask him. As the youngest member of the team, he has the world by the tail, and a date every night of the week. Leaving him wide open to the team's ribbing. No one would ever know it's a role he plays to try to forget the woman who stole his heart years ago.

When Night Storm is called in to rescue a busload of kidnapped university students in the Mexican jungle, it's a mission Nic can sink his teeth into. That is until he finds out his high school sweetheart, the love who was ripped from him, is one of the hostages and all bets are off. Will he be able to save her before they finally have a shot at happiness?

1

SHUT UP.

Shut up.

Shut up.

Shut up.

Camilla Ross had always known that some of the people she went to school with didn't have the sense God gave a gnat, but she'd never known they didn't have *any* sense of self-preservation either.

She squeezed Roxanne's hand.

Hard.

"Hush," she whispered as quietly as she could.

"You can't do this, we're Americans!" Roxanne shouted.

"Bitch, tell them we can," the man with the automatic weapon said in Spanish. He shoved the rifle into the tour guide's ribs. Hard. The woman somehow maintained a smile.

"If you understand English, I think they would listen better if it came from you," she responded in Spanish, her tone conciliatory.

He slapped her across the mouth and she fell against the front seat of the bus, but she didn't lose her footing.

"Do as I say, bitch," he said fiercely. She wiped the blood off of her mouth with the back of her hand then turned back to the bus of passengers, who were mostly university students from the east coast of America. Some of the students had come to Mexico to party, some had come to take in the history of the country; none of the students had been prepared for this.

"Tell them to shut the fuck up," the man with the gun said again.

"Everybody needs to remain calm and be quiet," the tour guide said loudly to all of the bus passengers.

Camilla looked out the window and saw that their bus was surrounded. There were three Jeeps and at least ten men.

"What's he saying?" Travis demanded to know. "Tell him to speak English for Christ's sake."

Travis was a football player for Penn State. He had been trying to get Roxanne to notice him since the tour had begun.

"Shut up," the scary man with the gun said in English as he took three steps down the middle of the bus. He stared down at Travis.

Travis stood up. "Make me."

The man casually hit Travis in the side of the head with the butt of his rifle. Travis slid down past his seat, onto the floor of the bus.

Did he kill him?

Two screams ricocheted through the bus, one from Roxanne.

"Anybody else?" the man asked in heavily accented English.

People started to cry and whimper.

"What do you want from us?" Roxanne asked.

"Money," he answered Roxanne in English. He turned to the tour guide whose mouth was still bleeding. "Tell her that if she is not silent I will find other uses for her," he said in Spanish.

"Roxanne, you need to be quiet, or he'll hurt you," Lisa Garcia said as she swiped at the blood running down her chin.

Camilla squeezed Roxanne's hand even tighter because she knew what the man had really said and what he really meant. The younger woman needed to shut the hell up.

Roxanne tried to pull away from Camilla's grip. When she couldn't she glared at Camilla. "Let go of me," she hissed.

Travis groaned from the floor.

Thank God.

Another man came onto the bus and pulled the bus driver out of his seat.

"I won't tell anybody, anything. I swear." The bus driver whimpered in Spanish.

"Get rid of him," the man with the gun said.

The second man dragged the bus driver out of the vehicle while he continued to beg and plead for his life. Camilla watched outside her window as the man shoved the bus driver to his knees. He looked terrified. Camilla thought she might throw up when a man in a green t-shirt casually lifted a pistol to the back of the nice old man's head and pulled the trigger. She slammed her eyes shut, but it wasn't in time to stop seeing the spray of blood and gore.

Our Father, Who art in heaven, please bless that kind man...

She swallowed and swallowed again. Continuing to say

prayers in her head for the man who had just been joking with them an hour ago.

"They killed him," the young man behind her murmured.

"He's dead," another girl in front of her sobbed softly.

Both of these students now realized the level of danger they were all in.

When she was finally able to open her eyes again, she glanced over at Roxanne who was still looking at the first gunman. She was giving him a typical look of brash defiance. Hadn't she heard the gunshot?

Camilla glanced around the rest of the bus. There were fifteen undergrads and graduate students on the bus, she was the only one working on her doctoral degree. That made her and the tour guide the old ladies on the bus because they were both at least twenty-four. So fifteen prisoners in all.

They'd been touring together for a day and a half. Camilla knew half of these people because she went to school with them at William and Mary College in Virginia. The rest she had just met. She knew that some of the students came from monied backgrounds, but how had these mercenaries known? Who exactly were they?

Roxanne pulled her phone out of the cross-body purse that she had been toying with for most of the bus ride.

"Put it back," Camilla said under her breath.

Roxanne glared at her, and twisted it around in a vain attempt to get a signal.

Camilla looked up to see if the gunman noticed, but he'd been distracted by two more men boarding the bus. She didn't know how it was possible, but they looked even scarier than the first man. She knew it was hopeless, but she looked over at Lisa for some sign of reassurance. Stunned, Camilla was met with an encouraging half-smile. It was as if Lisa were trying to tell her it was all going to be all right. For just a moment Camilla clung to that smile, even returning it with a nod. Maybe she had found someone she could rely on in this disaster.

The first man grabbed a hunk of Lisa's long dark hair and jerked her head back, baring her throat. He yelled in her face, spittle flying. "What are you smiling about? There's nothing to smile about," he roared in Spanish.

"I always smile when I'm scared, I can't help it. I'm sorry, please don't hit me again," Lisa begged.

"I won't hit you, beautiful, I promise." his voice turned seductive. Camilla shivered, and Lisa's eyes widened even further, her fear palpable. He pulled out a knife instead and casually sliced down her bare arm, from her bicep to her elbow.

"Anybody else want to smile?" The man yelled in English to the passengers. "Do you want to laugh?" He shoved Lisa to one of the other men who grabbed her around her bleeding arm. She let out a high shriek of pain.

"I'm the boss of you. Call me Boss. Do any of you speak Spanish?" Three people raised their hands, but Camilla didn't.

"Those of you who speak Spanish can call me *El Jefe*." He laughed as he strode down the aisle. When he came to Camilla's row, he looked at Roxanne and smiled. Roxanne gave him a tentative smile in return. He punched her, knocking her into Camilla.

"I told you not to smile," he yelled.

He turned and looked around the bus. "Does anyone else feel like smiling?"

Up front, two tears tracked down Lisa's face and blood from the knife wound trickled to the floor. She was no longer held by one of the mercenaries, so she was holding her arm, her hand doing nothing to staunch the flow of blood.

Roxanne was wailing in Camilla's arms like the world was coming to an end. Camilla thanked God that the punch had hit the back of her head; it could have been so much worse. She kept Roxanne cradled in her arms as she took another glance up to the front. Was Lisa bleeding even more profusely?

"Listen up, I need all of your purses, wallets, and phones. Your parents are going to pay money for all of you."

He went to the front of the bus and leaned out, "Maria," he shouted. "Get in here. I need you to start taking their information."

Of course, the boss had a secretary.

Camilla winced at her internal joke. Lisa might smile when she was scared, Camilla made jokes. She'd better stop it.

How about the one where my parents don't have a pot to piss in and I'm going to die? Is that funny?

Roxanne turned her head to look up at her. "He can't take my phone, I need it." Roxanne's whisper was frantic. She handed it to Camilla.

Camilla realized her own phone would be easily found in her purse on the floor, but having Roxanne's phone could be a real advantage later on. She turned it off, bent over Roxanne like she was giving aid, then shoved the phone down deep into her bra; for once her large bra cups coming in handy for something.

"Maria," the man shouted again.

Camilla looked out the window for Maria. She was a tall,

striking woman who walked with an air of authority. When Camilla saw her casually step over the corpse of the bus driver as if he were nothing more than a log, she knew that Maria was just as hard and evil as the rest of the men. The woman boarded the bus.

"You called?" she smiled at the boss.

"I need everyone on the bus tagged. Let's see how much people are willing to pay for the cattle."

She glanced dismissively at Lisa. "You cut her, so she's not important, right?"

"Tour guide. She might be able to help keep them calm. If not, you know what happens to her."

Lisa stood up straighter, a determined look on her face. El Jefe ignored her and continued to talk to Maria.

"Make them identify which packs are theirs and go through them." Once again he sauntered down the middle aisle and chose another two students to harass. They were a couple from Camilla's school. They were part of the reason she was here, Roxanne's and four other parents had pitched in to pay for her 'adventure' if she'd try to pound some knowledge into their babies while they were having fun in Mexico.

The boss banged open the luggage compartment over Paul and Jan's heads and grabbed a duffel bag and a backpack as they fell out.

"These yours?"

When the young man refused to answer, the girl gave a tentative nod. "Maria, start with them. I want to know everything."

Maria eased around the boss and grabbed the luggage from him. She threw the duffel at the man's head. He barely caught it before it hit him. She did the same thing to the girl with her backpack. She grunted when it hit the side of her face. Jan was doing the right thing, not bringing attention to herself.

"Come with me," Maria's voice was monotone. Paul helped Jan to stand up. He picked up her backpack.

"She can carry it," Maria told the young man.

"Let me." Jan took the backpack out of Paul's hands and followed Maria with Paul behind her. Camilla watched as Jan fell backward into Paul when she saw the dead bus driver.

"Quit your whining and follow me."

Once again Maria stepped over the dead body, but Paul led Jan around the corpse and they continued to follow Maria until she went to where a tarp was laid out on the ground.

Camilla couldn't hear what was being said, but the two students started to empty out the contents of their luggage onto the tarp.

"What do you find so interesting? Eh?"

Camilla looked up and saw the boss glaring down at her.

"What is so interesting?" he demanded to know.

Roxanne dug in deeper into Camilla's lap, trying to make herself as small a target as possible.

"I wanted to see what your friend was doing with Jan and Paul," Camilla answered in English.

"You better concentrate on what's happening here on the bus." He turned to Roxanne. "And you. Why are you hiding?" He yanked Roxanne's ponytail so that Roxanne was forced to sit up. Then he twisted it in his fist so that she was facing him.

"Leave me alone," she spat in a short burst of defiance.

He laughed.

"You're stupid, you know that, right? Do you like being

hit? Maybe you want to leave the bus now and be hit a few more times? Eh?"

"Please, she's young. She'll be quiet, I promise," Camilla pleaded.

"Ah, her protector. How interesting."

2

"Yo, you're not keeping up. You're young; what's your problem, another late night?"

Nic flipped Cullen Lyons, his Navy SEAL teammate, the finger and put on some serious speed as he clambered up the rope netting and swung over to the other side. At least now he had a fighting chance of coming in third on the obstacle course today.

Cullen was right, normally he would have come in second behind Ezio because there was just no stopping that guy these days. But no, Raiden was beating him, and Cullen was giving him a run for his money. Then there was Zed Zaragoza, who was catching up to him, and that guy was just coming off of disability leave!

Yeah, I seriously suck.

Nic pushed on, determined to come in second as he picked up speed. Two obstacles later when they were doing a low crawl through mud, Nic laughed at Cullen.

"Tough keeping up, isn't it old man? Have you gained some weight since Carys started cooking for you?"

Cullen snorted. "You think she cooks for me? You must be delusional, Son."

"Sorry, can't hear you, you're too far behind me," Nic shouted. He got up as soon as he was free of the short wire that they had to crawl under. He took a moment to look back. Cullen was almost done, but Zed was just halfway through.

Good!

Six more obstacles to go.

He ran up the hill at top speed then grabbed the weighted pack and shoved it up on his shoulder. He heard Cullen's *'oomph'* behind him.

"You're making old-man noises, Lyons."

"Fuck you, Hale."

Nic laughed and ran faster up the hill, but he could still see Cullen in his peripheral vision. The man was like a tick, he couldn't shake him off. The good news was that he was gaining on Raiden Sato.

He could see the high step coming up. Nothing more fun than running through tires without tripping. Hell, did the Navy get a kickback from Goodyear? Sure seemed to be more tires than the last time he'd run this course.

Nic chuckled when he saw Cullen trip.

"You're showing your age. What, are your knees giving out?" Nic taunted.

Once again Cullen gave him the finger. "You keep doing that Cullen and I'm going to think you're issuing an invitation."

"There is something just plain wrong with you, Nicholas Hale. I'm going to tell your Mama." Cullen was breathing hard.

Nic chuckled and left Cullen behind him. He saw the

walls coming up, each one higher than the next. He made a jump, then hoisted himself over the first wall. Did the same for the second. The third wall was evil; he had to jump three times before his fingers were able to grab onto the top of the wall. That's what happened when you were only six feet tall. He scrabbled up the wall and made it over.

Close to the end, he needed to haul ass to the next obstacle.

He took less than a second to look up at the spinning monkey bars that hung over a huge mud puddle. This was going to be simple. He'd been practicing that at the gym. This should be the point he really gained on Raiden. He saw him near the end of the obstacle course, still not done.

Nic climbed the netting up to the first hanging bars and jumped for it, he caught it with one hand and it twirled. He grabbed tight with his other hand and barely held on—but he did—then using his momentum he swung and caught the next damned spinning bar. On and on it continued. He never looked at Raiden or thought about Cullen; all he did was concentrate on the task at hand. He was in the zone. Before he knew it he was at the netting on the other side.

Raiden was just beginning to run from the base of that obstacle.

I crushed it!

"Great job, Nic!" Cullen yelled.

He practically slid down the netting and did a full-speed run to try to catch up with Raiden. He knew that Raiden was faster, so Nic would have to give it his all. Maybe carrying the weights at the next part of the obstacle course would give Nic some leverage.

It started to rain. *More mud to look forward to.* But only a couple more obstacles.

He was right; he did gain on Raiden a little bit, but still not enough to really make a dent on the man's lead.

Shit, at this rate, I'm still only going to come in third!

When Nic looked up he groaned. It was the ship boarding obstacle. A flimsy ladder, eight inches across and twenty feet high. You had to climb the damn thing, ring the bell, and come down. Raiden was going to nail this one. He was the most nimble of all the Night Storm team members.

Damn. Damn. Damn.

Nic did what he could, but with his size-twelve boot, he was screwed. The good news was that Cullen had the same damn problem. The bad news was that Raiden was already up the ladder and had rung the bell.

Asshole.

Raiden grinned at him as he basically slid down the ladder.

"Gotta up your game, Kid," Raiden said as he jumped off the ladder and hauled ass toward the next obstacle.

Nic went up the next ten feet and rang the bell, then he slid down. He didn't care about the pain in his palms, he was bound and determined to beat Raiden. He was sick and tired of being called Kid. He was twenty-fucking-four years old for fuck's sake.

The next obstacle was partly to Raiden's advantage and partly to Nic's. Being the ballerina that Raiden was, he could easily tiptoe up the logs to the steel wall. The asshole also had the upper body strength to lift himself up and over, but Nic had the height advantage, so...

Suck it, Raiden!

Nic didn't sweat as he went up the logs. His big feet kept him steady, if not fast. He easily went up and over the wall, even though it was narrow.

He raced down the log on the other side and jumped

down two steps ahead of Raiden. Hell, he didn't even see Ezio ahead. There was no chance of beating him, but still, he intended to beat Raiden with authority and leave Cullen sucking wind like the old man that he was. Hell, he was almost thirty-one!

Now it was more logs, and he was home free. He ran toward the obstacle full tilt and took a running jump. He was almost on top of the first one, then he took the momentum to rocket up to the second higher log. The third one was a Hail Mary, so he took a power jump and caught it, then hefted over and hit the ground, keeping his knees bent.

Now he could finally see Ezio. He was on the other side of the finish line, with a shit-eating grin on his face. *Asshole.* Nic would bet anything that he'd broken the course record.

He put his head down and ran.

Ran hard.

He saw the chalk line as he crossed it, and started to slow and circle back.

"'Bout time. What took you so long?" Ezio shouted out. "I thought you were young and healthy? Is your social life finally taking a toll?"

Nic ignored him and went over to the rucksack that held bottles of water. God, he was thirsty. He looked up as Raiden crossed the finish line, so he pulled out two more bottles. Nic chuckled when Cullen shouted out a '*Goddammit, I didn't even podium.*'

Ezio laughed the hardest.

"I saw what you ate for dinner last night, man. There wasn't a chance in hell that you were going to place in the top three today. Unless of course Nic here didn't get a wink of sleep, drank a quart of whisky, and smoked three packs of Camels."

"Fuck you, Ezio. I didn't eat that much," Cullen protested.

Ezio let out an easy laugh. "Samantha cooked a brisket and all the trimmings and you guys fell on it like ravening wolves. You can tell that Carys and A.J. don't cook."

"We would have got in trouble, except for the fact that Carys and A.J. plowed in just as much as we did," Cullen laughed.

"I don't get it," Nic said. "Samantha's cooking is great, so why did you win, Ezio?"

"I've been feasting on it for the last three months. I now understand moderation," Ezio grinned. "Which apparently you do too, if you came in second. So it wasn't a big date night for you? No staying out all night?"

Nic kept his mouth shut. He had stayed out all night, but he sure as hell wasn't going to explain to his teammates what he had been doing; it would have been bad for his rep. Speaking of which, at this rate, he was going to be late.

Kane came over the line next, followed by Asher.

"Where's Leo?" Zed asked. "He never comes in last. "Sorry, McNamara, but it's you. Your brains don't translate to the Kraken; that one fucks you up each and every time. Thank God you're so good at brute force."

Everyone laughed.

"The sad thing is, I practiced that damned cargo net piece of shit obstacle five times this week." Kane threw down his empty water bottle. "That does it; I'm recreating that obstacle at my house. I'm done letting that thing own my ass."

Nic shot Raiden an amused look.

"I saw that, Hale. Just for that, you're stuck bringing nothing but your mother's cooking to the next party I throw.

I don't care how much you have to beg to get her to cook, I expect blackberry cobbler at the very least."

Shit, I'm screwed, I really need to learn how to bake.

I'M LATE. I hate being late.

The door opened before Nic had a chance to knock. "You're late."

"We had to run the obstacle course today. I'm begging you, cut me some slack," he said as he held up his hands for mercy. The beautiful blonde smiled, then he scowled. "There's a peephole for a reason, you know the rules."

"Don't be grouchy. Please." She batted her eyelashes up at him. It was a worthy ploy, because Nic felt himself melting.

"Mimi, you need to be more cautious."

"It's Saturday. It's always you." She held out her hand so he could hold it.

"I don't care. You're not allowed to open the door without checking the peephole." There had been one installed at her height for just that reason.

"You're a poopy-head."

"Naomi! You won't speak to Uncle Nic that way. If you do, he'll have to leave."

Nic and Mimi looked up to see an older version of Mimi coming out of the kitchen with a frown. She was not happy.

"I'm sorry, Mom."

"Am I the one who you have to apologize to? Where did you learn such awful language?"

Mimi tugged at Nic's hand so that he would crouch down beside her wheelchair. "I'm sorry for calling you a poopy-head, Nic. You're not. Your hair is nice."

Laughter bubbled up inside him but he had to keep it contained or Alice would come down on him like a ton of bricks. She did not cotton to bad manners from her six-year-old daughter. Naomi 'Mimi' Daniels was treated just like any other girl her age...well almost. His cousin was doing a fantastic job, except for the fact that she was trying to be all things to all people and she was grinding herself into the dirt.

"I like your hair too." Nic smiled at Mimi. "Now let me take the groceries into the kitchen. I have a project planned for today."

He saw Alice frown. *Uh-oh.* Now he was going to suffer the wrath. "I had to bring groceries because it's part of the project. We're making blackberry cobbler." He wouldn't tell her he brought over extra.

"You're going to bake?" Alice's voice was filled with surprise.

"Don't act so surprised. I can bake."

Alice's laughter filled the foyer and Mimi joined in. "Why are we laughing at Uncle Nic?"

"If you're helping him bake tonight, you'll see soon enough, Lovebug." Alice kissed the top of her daughter's head.

"Give me a break, it's not going to be that bad," Nic said.

"You couldn't even peel the potatoes to Aunt Scarlett's specifications, what are you talking about?" Alice scoffed.

"Is Auntie Scarlett coming over?" Mimi asked. Aside from her Uncle Nic, his mother was one of her favorite people.

"Not today, you're stuck with just me." He tweaked the little girl's nose and she giggled. He loved her giggle. It sounded like bells.

"You know, I could teach you—" Alice started.

"Don't even think about it. I know you have plans. Off you go, young woman. Where's your purse? Do you have your cell phone? Is it charged this time?"

"Yeah, Mom, it better be, otherwise Uncle Nic swears, and then he feels bad," Mimi said, looking up at her mother with a smirk.

"Great, now I have both of you ganging up on me. That's so not fair."

Nic looked at Alice. Really looked at her. He could see the signs of strain around her mouth, and the bruising under her eyes from lack of sleep and probably worry. He hated that. He wished he could do more, but she refused to take anything she considered a handout. She was determined to handle things on her own. Stubborn. The woman was stubborn. But at least he had convinced her to let him take care of Mimi once a week while she took time for herself. It had taken a year of coercion to make it happen, but he'd done it.

"Alice, you're going to be late," he said softly.

"I know, I know." She reached up and kissed his cheek. She crouched down in front of Mimi. "You're going to be a good girl for Uncle Nic, right?"

"Yes, Mom, I promise."

"I love you bunches and bunches and bunches."

Mimi threw her arms wide and Alice pulled her frail body into a hug.

"Remember to make Uncle Nic clean up after himself." Alice grinned at Mimi.

"I will."

Alice headed for the door, giving her child one last long look.

Damn, Nic hadn't talked to Alice since the last time he'd been here. Had something gone wrong that he wasn't aware of? Alice had some 'splaining to do when she got home tonight.

"You ready to bake?" he asked the little girl.

Her blonde curls bounced as she nodded. "Okay, let's unpack the groceries. There's more in the car that I'll have to bring in."

"Okay. I can help," she gave a huge smile.

"I'm counting on it."

"WHAT'S THAT AWFUL SMELL?" Alice asked as she opened the front door. Her nose twitched the same way her daughter's had after the first burnt offering.

"Be glad you weren't here at four o'clock. Now that it's eleven o'clock the smell has dissipated."

"It's godawful. Aunt Scarlett was right never to let you in the kitchen."

"Yeah, but I succeeded. There's cobbler in the kitchen."

Alice followed him into the kitchen and burst out laughing. "Honey, this is not cobbler, where's the crust?"

"There's some at the bottom, I swear."

Alice hip-checked him to get to the silverware drawer and took out a fork, then she casually dipped it into his masterpiece.

"Hey, aren't you going to get a plate or a bowl or something?" He asked as she tasted the cobbler.

"This isn't bad. A little runny, but it tastes like cobbler."

"Come on, it's the third time I made cobbler, be kind," he said as he pulled out a spoon and a bowl then headed to the freezer and grabbed a quart of vanilla ice cream.

"When did you make a cobbler before?" Alice asked as she greedily grabbed the ice cream out of his hands.

"Earlier today. This was my third attempt."

Alice's laugh sounded like Mimi's, a beautiful sound. Too bad she didn't laugh all that often.

"You baked three cobblers? Where are the other two?"

"They ended up in the trash," Nic said as he scooped up two bowls of runny blackberry goo and smothered them in vanilla ice cream.

"That's such a waste. Wait a minute, where did the ice cream come from?"

Before Alice sat down at the table, she went back to the refrigerator and opened the freezer.

"Dammit Nic, I told you not to buy groceries for me. That is not part of our deal."

"My deal is that I'm a growing boy, and I need man food here when I come over to watch Mimi. You have girl food, it doesn't work for me."

She pulled out frozen pork chops, hamburger patties, and a rib roast. "Just how often do you intend to come over? There's enough to feed your whole unit."

"Team, we're a team, not a unit," he clarified after he swallowed his blackberry-flavored ice cream.

"Whatever." She shoved the meat back into the freezer, then opened the fridge and growled.

"Come over to the table, your ice cream is melting."

"Goddammit, Nic. You're pissing me off," she said as she stomped over to the table and flounced into the chair.

"Join the club. You've been pissing me off for the last year. This is not a damned handout. If the positions were reversed, you'd be doing the same damned thing. One day they probably will be reversed and I'm going to need a hand, so this is my way of buying into your good graces."

She slid a large portion of dessert into her mouth, and Nic knew it was so she didn't have to talk. She was definitely pissed. Well, she'd just have to suck it up. She needed the help. Things were tight for her right now, and that fuck-nut of an ex-husband still wasn't paying child support, so Nic was going to help where he could.

"I don't like this, Nic."

"I know you don't, Allie," he said using the nickname from their childhood. "But this isn't just about you, it's about Mimi. You know that, I know you do."

"She never goes without!" Alice was shocked.

"No, but her mother does, and that's just as bad. You don't think Mimi sees that? You don't think your losing weight and lack of energy doesn't affect that little girl? I know you're banking on that promotion, and I know you, you'll get it. But in the meantime, you need some help. Take it. Take it from Mom and Dad, too."

He saw tears fill her eyes.

"I just thought I could handle this, you know?"

"I don't know how. Most couples couldn't handle this with two salaries, and two sets of hands. It's time you let us help. You're breaking Mom's heart, she thinks of you as the daughter she never had."

Alice pushed her bowl of ice cream away and crossed her arms on the table, then rested her head on it. "You promise I'm not a failure?" she whispered.

"I promise. Shit, Alice, the only failure in this sad scenario is your deadbeat ex-husband, and as soon as he's located, he'll be taken care of."

Her head jerked up and she gave him a worried look. "What are you talking about?"

"Nothing you need to concern yourself with."

"Okay, if it's nothing I need to concern myself with, then

I won't." She pulled back her melted ice cream and sipped a bit from her spoon. "Let's turn the tables for a second. How about you? I don't see your life being all put together. Care to have a sharing circle?"

"What are you talking about? I'm fine. I have my friends, I have an active social life. Work is great. I'm getting my kid-fix with Mimi."

"Which you don't tell anyone about, instead you let your friends," she said friends in air quotes, "think that you're out gallivanting around the nights you're babysitting for me. What's the deal, Nic? Why are you trying to sound like more of a horndog than you actually are?"

He took his bowl back to the counter and scooped up more cobbler then grabbed more ice cream out of the freezer. "Want some?" he asked Alice.

"Nope, I want answers."

"You and me both," he muttered.

"Nope. That's not going to cut it. You're smarter than that. You make me do a deep-dive on my psychosis, so you can return the favor. What the hell is going on?"

He looked into green eyes, so like his own, and sighed. "Can I say that the whole man-whore thing has gotten old and leave it at that?"

She shot him a steady stare and he knew that she wasn't going to let him get away with that answer either. "I still have to do better?" he chuckled. "You're tough."

"It's in our DNA. I have my suspicions, I just want to see if you can get past all that SEAL training and figure out what's going on in your heart."

Nic held up his hands. "Hey, hey, hey. Who said anything about my heart being involved? I'm just growing up. I'm sick of transitory relationships."

"That's a big ole load of crap. Those were the only kind

of relationships you looked for after high school. If a woman with potential showed up in your world, you ran away faster than an Olympic athlete. But if there was a woman who was only interested in your reputation as a SEAL, or your muscles, *then* you showed some interest."

"That isn't true; some of those women were really nice."

Alice snorted into her ice cream. "They had more notches on their bedposts than you did. You didn't do nice." Once again she used air quotes around the word *do*.

Nic winced. It was true.

"Well, that was then, this is now. Now I'm not much interested in anything."

"Oh, you're celibate?" She arched an eyebrow.

"What, only women are allowed to try that on for size? You've told me yourself that you haven't been into relationships or anything else since Don left. Why is it so hard to believe that I've hit a dry spell?"

Alice sighed and put her hand on his forearm.

"Do you think you're finally over her? It's been six years. Can you move on?"

"I don't know. Maybe." He stood up and put his bowl in the sink. "Are you done with yours?"

Alice nodded and he put hers in the sink too. Then he reached for the blackberry cobbler pan.

"What are you doing with that?" she asked quickly.

"I figured the trash."

"Well, stop figuring. That was pretty tasty with ice cream. I'm going to put some Saran Wrap on it and put it in the fridge. So why the need to bake?"

"I owe one of the guys Mom's cobbler at the next cookout, thought I'd try baking my own."

Alice laughed, then opened the fridge. She pulled out the remaining baskets of berries that he had left. "I tell you what. I've got you covered. That way you don't have to ask Aunt Scarlett."

He perked up. "That'd be great! I'll owe you."

"Like hell you will," she said as she batted him on the back of the head.

His laugh bellowed across the kitchen.

3

"WHERE ARE WE?" ROXANNE ASKED FOR THE FOURTH TIME. Camilla looked out the window into the dark jungle. All she could see was black, with occasional shots of green when the lights from one of the Jeeps that was following them shone on the foliage.

How often was she going to ask the same damn question?

Camilla ignored the girl's question this time.

"Camilla, answer me. Where do you think we are?" She sounded like she was talking to a servant.

"Roxanne, you need to stop talking. And for the last time, we're in the Mexican jungle," she said in the lowest whisper she could.

"When are they going to let us go?"

Camilla had already tried not answering her questions, but that just caused Roxanne to ask more questions, faster and louder. The girl could *not* stop talking. El Jefe was going to single her out again, for sure.

Camilla turned in her seat and gripped Roxanne's thigh, hard. "Do. Not. Speak."

Suddenly, Roxanne's eyes filled with tears.

Camilla loosened her grip and leaned into the girl so she was talking directly into her ear. "These men are savages. We don't know what they're capable of. Roxanne, you're young and pretty, I don't want them noticing you. You need to keep *quiet*."

Understanding dawned at long last in Roxanne's eyes. She whispered back. "I talk when I'm scared. I always have."

Camilla gave her best student-teacher encouraging smile. "Now's a good time to learn a new habit. I know you can, Roxanne. I believe in you."

"You do?" Her blue eyes sparked with hope.

"I do," Camilla said fervently.

Please God, let her learn.

They'd been on the road for over eight hours. The one bathroom break they'd had, had been awful. Peeing behind a tree in the jungle wasn't her idea of fun, but having to do it when leering males were mere feet away was almost the worst experience of her life. When she and Lisa had finished, they'd done what they could to shield some of the other young women from prying eyes. Their captors had laughed at their attempts.

Camilla knew deep in her heart this was going to get worse before it was going to get better, so her job was to help keep her 'kids' safe. Roxanne was one of the weakest links. She'd been taking headcount around the bus to determine who else was likely to be singled out. There was Travis Driver—he'd already had one run-in with El Jefe, and Camilla knew that he was going to be looking for a chance to prove himself against their captors. If he fought again, he'd probably be killed. There had to be a way for her to convince him to stand down.

Then there was Phyllis Agar—she was a hard one to pin down. Like Roxanne, she came from a background of extreme wealth, but she never flaunted it. Somehow she was a girl who was always on the outside looking in, and she seemed to be ostracized by everyone, which meant that no one would be willing to help her if it came down to it.

Camilla was also worried about Lisa Garcia. She was from Tempe, Arizona, and they had developed a friendship on the first day. She'd already heard the leader talk about the fact that she wasn't worth any money to them, so she was disposable. Camilla *had* to make it seem like Lisa was an integral part of this groups' cooperation. Perhaps she could—

Her head slammed forward, only to be jerked back by the strap of her seatbelt. Her head smashed into the seat rest behind her like it been shot out of a gun. Her mouth opened to scream in pain, but no sound came out. She jerked forward again like a ragdoll. Back and forth she went until her head hung down and she wondered if her neck was broken.

Her ears were ringing; she couldn't hear anything but the sound of the loud clang.

Wait. That wasn't ringing. That was crying and screams.

When she finally heaved a sigh of relief because her body was still, she felt her body begin to fall sideways toward Roxanne. She could barely turn her head, it hurt so much, but she managed it. Roxanne's eyes were closed.

Camilla looked past the unconscious girl and saw luggage falling onto Liz and Brian who were in the seat across from her. The window that Liz was sitting next to was broken, and a tree branch was sticking through it. The branch was covered in blood. *Liz's blood!*

The bus is on its side!

She could barely move her head from the pain but she prayed as hard as she could that she would see El Jefe sprawled dead across the aisle since he hadn't been buckled in. Inch by slow inch, she turned her neck so that she could see near the front of the bus, but there was no sign of El Jefe. Finally, she spotted Lisa. She was hanging out of the seat behind the driver's seat. Apparently, she only had a lap seat belt. *Dammit!*

"Roxanne, can you hear me?" she prodded the girl beside her.

She didn't respond.

Camilla lifted her hand and touched her fingers to Roxanne's neck. A swoosh of air left her lungs as she sighed in relief. Roxanne's pulse was fine. She heard others in the bus beginning to talk to one another, asking their status. She looked over and saw Brian trying to get Liz to respond. He wasn't having any success.

"Doctor Ross!" a voice called out to her from the back of the bus. Camilla recognized who was talking. It was Michael Lyton, one of the football players from William and Mary College. He was only a sophomore, but he had a good head on his shoulders.

"What's going on, Michael?"

"Can you come here? It's important."

"I'm basically hanging from the ceiling, Michael. I can't get there." She turned her body so that she could see over the tall bus seat and look toward the back of the bus as best she could.

Oh, God.

"Michael, don't. The other men will be boarding the bus any minute," she begged the young man. He had El Jefe's rifle. The kidnapper was sprawled unconscious across two seats, and Michael had the rifle pointed at El Jefe's temple.

"I'm not going to kill him, I'm going to use him as a way

to get us out of here. They won't want their leader dead. Will they?"

It was the way he asked the question, 'will they' that got her attention. It scared her to think that she was somehow the leader in this fiasco, and if she didn't do something, Michael was going to end up dead because he tried to outgun the kidnappers.

"Michael, drop the gun, it's a losing proposition."

"No, it's not. You're doing good, man," Travis yelled out.

"Be quiet, Travis. You're not helping," she gritted out loudly. "Michael, stop this before he wakes up."

"If he wakes up, I'll kill him. He's the leader: without him, maybe the others will let us go."

"He's the one keeping the others in line. It would be worse without him," she argued.

"Don't listen to her. We need him as a hostage," Travis interjected.

To hell with El Jefe, I'm going to kill Travis!

Camilla could hear clamoring outside the bus. They were being boarded. She turned her head toward the bus door and saw Travis letting himself out of his seat and dropping down so that he could join Michael.

"Gentlemen, you're going to get killed. Stop this now." She used her best student-teacher voice.

"Shut up, Doctor Ross, this isn't the classroom," Travis bellowed.

Before he could reach Michael, El Jefe's hand moved and grabbed the barrel of the rifle. He pulled it forward as he moved his head, forcing it to go past him. A shot fired into the seat that the kidnapper had been lying across. Blood splattered against the far window as Larry Collins was shot in the head.

Camilla closed her eyes against the horrifying scene. How would Michael ever live with himself?

"Jesus. God no." Travis sounded like he was in intense pain.

Camilla opened her eyes and looked at Travis, who was staring at Michael. She turned to look at Michael and gasped in horror for a second time. El Jefe's knife stuck out of Michael's neck. For just an instant Michael's eyes sought hers out. They connected, he saw her, he was pleading for something. Anything.

Oh God, the terror and pain on that boy's face as he looks at me. I can't look away, I need to be strong for him.

Camilla's heart wrenched as she watched the life fade out of his eyes before he slumped to the floor.

El Jefe, who now had the rifle, shot a long burst of bullets into the bus's side that was now acting as the ceiling. "Who else wants to try something stupid?" he roared as he staggered toward the front of the bus. Travis, who was still standing in what was now the middle aisle, held up his hands.

"I don't want any trouble. I promise."

El Jefe jabbed the tip of the rifle into Travis' stomach, causing the young man to gasp with pain. "Are you rich? How much will your parents pay for you?"

"A lot," Travis promised.

"Enough for you and the two kids who died? Including the one you forced me to kill? Because his death is on you." Travis looked like he was going to throw up. "Your parents' ransom will be three times as much as all the others. If they don't pay, my men will tie you to a tree and leave you for the jaguars. You understand me?"

Travis didn't say anything.

This time El Jefe heaved the rifle backward, and

pounded the gun into Travis' stomach, slamming the kid so hard that he skidded along the side of the bus, through the broken glass. No screams this time, only whimpers came from the other students.

El Jefe picked him up by his shirt collar and flung him sideways, out of his path, so that he could make his way to the front of the bus. That was the first time Camilla noticed that the door to the bus was open and some of the other kidnappers were crawling inside.

"How many dead?" one of the men asked.

"I don't know, do a count," the leader said as he stepped by Lisa and looked down at the semi-conscious driver. He grabbed his hair and jerked his head around so that his face was looking up at El Jefe. "You fucked up."

Camilla shut her eyes. She heard screams and knew that the man was dead.

NIC HAD HAD a hard time sleeping the night before—too many dreams of pain and loss. Nothing new. Missions where people were wounded or died got confused with the last time he saw her face. Her tears and that last gut-wrenching goodbye. It was nights like that when he just got up and trained until his muscles were on fire. Until he couldn't think about anything else.

Now here he was in a briefing, paying for it, his concentration shot.

He sucked down another large gulp of coffee laden with sugar, praying it would wake him up. Two nights in a row of non-existent sleep were taking their toll.

"—likely to saddle up. We just need a little more intel as to which way they went after the initial take-down.

Unfortunately with the tree canopy being so thick, it's a crapshoot. We're depending on some of the locals on the ground. We're going to drop in."

Nic looked up from his coffee to see Asher and Cullen looking up in excitement. They were the ones who scored highest and jump school and always had shit-eating grins on their faces whenever they had to drop into a mission. Then Nic looked at Zed Zaragoza. He looked as calm as normal—that man always looked like he had taken a Xanax —but Nic couldn't help but be worried for him. He had recently come off of a catastrophic injury. Would he be up for the jump?

As if he could feel Nic's eyes on him, Zed turned around and lifted an eyebrow his way. Nic raised his coffee cup an inch in reply at being caught. Zed gave him a half-smile. That was all it took, and Nic felt reassured that Zed would be fine.

How can he read me so well? That man is scary with a capital 'S'.

"Have the parents at William and Mary College been notified? What about the others?" Kane asked Max.

"Negative. The only reason anyone has been alerted is that the tour guide got a message out before the bus was boarded. She kept a cool head and gave coordinates and said there were three Jeeps."

Nic figured that had to mean at least twelve men.

"As a local, she probably has knowledge about how this goes down," Leo said.

"Her name might be Lisa Garcia, but she's from Tempe, Arizona. She's as apple pie as the rest of us," Max explained. "The only local on the bus is the bus driver; everyone else by our estimation is American. The last time a kidnapping of

Americans like this has gone down was a year and a half ago, and it wasn't nearly this size."

"I thought they were kidnapping businessmen." Asher looked confused.

"I hate to say it, but those are getting to be a little too commonplace, and are onesy-twosies, that's why more and more companies have opted for kidnap, war, terrorism, and ransom insurance. A lot of the kidnappings that happen don't even make it to the military. This isn't the same thing. This is definitely *ours* to deal with."

"So, when did Lisa call out the coordinates?" Nic asked.

"Eighteen hours ago. They're going to try to get as far away from the capture zone as possible, as quick as possible."

"Where were they?"

Max hit the lights in the briefing room and Kane's projector flashed a picture of the Yucatan peninsula up on the screen at the front of the room. "This is almost smack dab between Chetumal and Calakmul. According to the tour company they were supposed to be visiting the Mayan ruins in Calakmul yesterday."

"They must be pretty studious college students if they were going to visit a bunch of ruins," Ezio commented.

"They were coming from three nights in Cancun. My guess is they were pretty hungover college students," Kane responded.

"Since the F.B.I is saying no ransom demands have been made, we've got to assume that they haven't reached their stopping point, because you sure as hell know they didn't stay put," Max interjected.

"That doesn't make sense," Cullen objected. "They probably have satellite phones; why not start making calls while they're on the road?"

"They need to figure out who they have, and who they need to call," Kane said emphatically.

Makes sense, Nic thought. But he couldn't stop thinking of William and Mary College. That's where Camilla had gone to school all those years ago when they had parted ways. Imagining young students like her on the bus, so innocent and scared, made him furious. Furious and scared. They had to get them the hell out of there.

"We still don't have the green light on this mission, but my gut tells me we will," Max was saying. "I want all of you on to stay near base, and be ready at the drop of a hat."

They all nodded.

4

Dawn in the jungle came as a blessed relief. She could finally see all of the others from the tour bus and make an assessment of their injuries. Why hadn't that bastard let them stay in the bus instead of sleeping on the bug-infested jungle floor? She was positive that ants were literally in her pants, okay capris, but same difference. She'd squirm but that would only arouse the men's attention, which was the last thing she wanted.

Camilla knew that Michael, Larry, and Liz were dead, but as she did a headcount, there were only eleven students instead of fifteen. Who else was missing? She kept looking around the makeshift campsite, but couldn't see anyone else.

To hell with it, I'm getting up. So what if I wiggle?

Camilla eased away from Roxanne, working hard not to disturb her. Phyllis was on her other side. Her heart ached for the two girls. Neither of them was equipped to cope with this; hell, she wasn't equipped to cope with this, but she didn't have a choice but to pull up her ant-filled panties and deal.

Everyone was bunched together in a big dogpile, for comfort and safety. Mostly the girls and guys had separated with a few exceptions. Besides Phyllis and Roxanne, Pam was wedged beside Lisa.

Camilla had spotted Paul and Jan snuggled together. She'd noted that Travis was sleeping the farthest away from the group. The couple of times she'd managed to fall asleep she'd replayed Michael and Larry's deaths and woke up muffling a scream. Camilla vacillated between ready to lunge at Travis or hug him because she knew how badly he must be hurting.

Not now.

She continued her headcount. The young men were close. She saw Brian Lane staring at her and finally found Wendy; she was a small girl and she was cuddled closely to his side. She knew that Michael and Liz were dead, so that left Haley.

"What are you doing?" a woman growled in accented English.

Camilla looked up and saw Maria advancing on her.

"I'm doing a headcount of my students."

"Headcount?"

"I'm checking to see if all of my students are here," Camilla clarified softly as Maria walked into her personal space.

"If they're not here, they're dead on the bus."

"There's only three people dead on the bus, and I'm missing one girl," Camilla said.

"You're wrong. There are two dead men and two dead women on the bus."

Camilla's legs turned to water. "Two women?" She grabbed Maria's arm. "Show me!"

Maria shook off her hand and shoved her face into

Camilla's. "Don't ever touch me again, bitch, or I'll hurt you so bad, nobody will recognize you when you go home. Do you understand me?"

Camilla stumbled backward.

"Please, can you show me the two girls? I know Liz was killed, but I thought she, Michael, and Larry were the only ones who died. I'm begging you," Camilla said as she pressed her palms together. She knew that there were tears in her eyes, but she didn't care. Let the woman see that she was vulnerable. Who cared? She was. Two young girls were dead!

"Make it quick, we're leaving as soon as the sun is up." Maria grabbed Camilla's arm and practically dragged her forward. Camilla was in pain from the crash but she thrust it aside and concentrated on getting to the bus. Then she tripped. Maria laughed. Camilla knew that the woman was taking pleasure in her stumble. The woman had sadistic tendencies.

When they got to the turned-over bus a man was leaning against it with his gun slung against his chest as he smoked a cigarette.

"Did you bring me a present?" he leered at Camilla as he addressed Maria in Spanish.

"Until we video them, nobody is going to rough them up, you know the drill," Maria said drily.

"I can make sure not to mark up her face."

"Shut up, you know the rules. Now open the door. She needs to identify the dead so we can make sure we know who to ransom."

The man hoisted himself up on the bus wheel so that he could get up to the door that was now up top. He leaned over and held out his hand. "Who first?"

"Her," Maria said in Spanish.

"Take his hand," Maria said to Camilla in English. "I'll hoist you up." Between the two of them, Camilla made it to the top of the rolled-over bus and sat next to the bus door. The man reached for Maria, but she pushed his hand away and climbed up using the tire as leverage. The sun was coming up but it was dark when Camilla looked down into the bus. Maria shone a flashlight.

"Come on," Maria said. Camilla watched as she dropped down into the mouth of the bus. "Drop her down to me, Raymundo."

Raymundo grabbed Camilla around her armpits and lowered her into the dark and Maria grabbed her feet. She helped Camilla the rest of the way down and arranged it so that she was standing on the side of a cargo bin.

"Follow me, but be careful."

The eerie glow of the flashlight pinged around the tomblike interior. Camilla carefully picked her way along the luggage racks and sides of chairs, trying to avoid the broken windows.

"Shit!"

"I told you to be careful!" Maria shouted as her flashlight swung around and found Camilla hanging onto a luggage rack as she tried to wrest her sneaker from in between two seats. Maria muttered in Spanish about uncoordinated cows as she grabbed Camilla's hand and started to guide her.

"Follow exactly in my footsteps."

Camilla did, and soon they got to the back of the bus, she moaned.

There was Haley.

Her body was crumpled at the bottom of the bus, her neck obviously broken.

"You know her?"

She crouched down to touch the young girl's hair. Two days ago Haley was telling her how excited she was to visit the Mayan ruin. She was one of the few students who was more into studying than partying. Haley's form swam in front of Camilla. She panicked as she couldn't make out the girl's features. It took her a moment to realize she was crying.

Maria gripped her shoulder and shook. "Answer the question. Do you know her?"

Camilla covered her mouth to smother a sob and nodded.

"Who is she?"

"Haley Anderson."

"Is she worth money?"

Camilla couldn't compute the question.

"Answer me. How much are her parents worth? Is she worth money?"

She rounded on Maria. "What does it matter? She's dead!"

Maria callously shoved at Haley's body, rolling her onto her stomach. "Help me look."

"What are you talking about?"

"Find her purse or something. Anything with contact information for her parents."

"She's dead," Camilla cried again. "Leave her alone."

Maria's hands dug under Haley's body and came up with a small satchel. "I found it," she said with glee. She dug into the tiny bag and pulled out a wallet, phone, and notebook. "Let's get out of here."

"What are you talking about? We need to bury her and the others," Camilla protested.

"We don't have time. We need to move today. Don't worry, they'll be taken care of. The cats need to eat."

The breath whooshed out of Camilla as she looked at Maria.

"You can't mean that."

Maria shrugged and started back toward the front of the bus.

Camilla grabbed her arm and swung her back. "We are not leaving them."

Maria's hand shot out and she backhanded Camilla hard across the face, sending her flying. She had to push against Haley's hip to get back up.

"I told you not to touch me, you stupid bitch," Maria bit out. "Do as I say and you might make it out of this alive."

Camilla followed Maria out of the bus.

NIC'S SLEEP was fraught with dreams. Everything that Alice had said stirred up old memories. All he could think about was the girl he had once loved with his whole heart. Who was he kidding, she was the woman he still loved. He hit his pillow and rolled over, willing himself to go back to sleep.

"SHHHH, it's going to be okay, Baby." Nic stroked his hand down her delicate back. This was the furthest they had ever taken things.

She looked up at him, her eyes sheened with tears. "I don't want to wait anymore," she whispered. Her trembling hand reached up to cup his cheek. "I'm not scared, Nic. I love you more than anything or anyone on this earth."

Nic's heart pumped up at least three sizes.

The lush feel of her naked breasts against his chest felt

sublime. Ever so slowly she undulated against him, and he felt her turgid nipples scrape against his skin. He groaned.

"Are you all right?" she whispered. He looked at her to see if she was teasing and found that she was sincerely worried about him.

He gave her the best smile that he was able to. "Move again a couple of times and let's find out."

Dawning comprehension lit up her face and she grinned as she shimmied against him once again. Nic had a strong sense of fairness, so he took one lush breast in his hand and thumbed her nipple, glorying in her moan of pleasure.

"Are you all right?" he asked with a devilish grin.

"Do it a few more times and I'll let you know." Her voice was a siren's song.

He did, again and again. His thumb swirled around her tightening bud until he couldn't stand it a minute longer. He swooped down and took the tip into his mouth and sucked.

She covered her mouth with the back of her wrist. There was no need. They were in his bed and no one was home. "I want to hear you."

Her chestnut hair drifted across his pillow as she shook her head. He went back and sucked harder. This time she let out a soft shriek. He smiled against her soft flesh. Camilla was everything to him.

"More, Nic. More." She moved so that her denim-covered legs rested on either side of his hips, nestling his erection against her core. If it hadn't been for their jeans, they'd be making love. She was driving him crazy.

He'd known Cami Ross for almost two years, but it had seemed like a lifetime. Everything about her enticed him, enthralled him, but there wasn't a chance in hell he was going to take this any further tonight or any other night until he put a ring on her finger. He wanted their future settled.

"You know the rules, our pants stay on," he whispered with a grimace.

"I don't like those rules anymore. They're stupid rules. I turned eighteen last month. We're graduating in three weeks. Those rules don't apply anymore."

Pushing a strand of hair behind her ear, he looked deep into her sky blue eyes. "Those rules do matter. It's a matter of honor. My honor matters to me. Your honor matters to me."

She bit her bottom lip. Cami did that when she was worried or thinking about something. If her fingers weren't tangled in his hair, she'd be twirling her own.

"I would never do anything that would have you do something that would break your code of honor," she said at last. "But what are we waiting for? Graduation?"

"You'll see, be patient." But even with their jeans on, he knew what he could do, Cami was so sensual and close to coming, that he could help her fly over the edge. It wouldn't take much. He kissed away the frown lines on her brow and she relaxed. His lips feathered down along her jaw, and her lips sought his. How could he resist the taste of her plump sweet lips? He lingered for an open-mouthed kiss that communicated so much. It was clear that their hearts belonged to one another.

One hand cupped her cheek while the other slid along the outside of her leg, coaxing it to wrap around his waist. He groaned into her mouth as he felt her heat through the layers of denim. He prayed that the steel of his zipper would hold, otherwise, he would burst through his jeans. He gripped her butt, the one that drove him insane when she walked in front of him. Once again Nic took the tip of her breast in his mouth but this time he gently raked it with her teeth and she pushed up against him.

"Holy hell."

He grinned. She rarely swore so he knew he was getting to her. Wait until she felt what was coming next.

Nic started a slow slide against her core, up and down, exactly matching the licks that he was now bestowing on her nipple. Sweat broke out on his forehead as he worked to maintain control.

"What are y-y-you doing?" she stuttered.

He didn't answer, he just continued. Up and down.

Stroke.

Lick.

Stroke.

Until she was moaning. Nic took a moment away from her breast so he could look into her eyes. Her irises had turned a dark navy, her gaze hazy with passion.

"Don't stop."

"I'm not."

Her hands shot up and gripped his hair, pulling his head back down toward her breast, mashing it close for a harder touch than before. Was there any man on earth who could have resisted? He took the rose-tipped nub into his mouth and sucked, twirling his tongue around her nipple. Her taste was exquisite.

Cami's grip changed; now she was petting his head, running her fingers through his hair, her nails driving him insane. The more she did it, the more his lower body lost its rhythm, and he found himself pushing against her uncontrollably.

Now she had both legs clutched around him as she worked in tandem with each movement.

I'm going to lose it. I haven't lost control since I was thirteen!

Her sighs and moans intermingled with her pleas.

"Nic...please," she begged in a husky tone that didn't sound like her at all. She clutched him harder, and he fell under her spell —all he could think about was giving her pleasure. Anything

that would physically convey what mere words couldn't. After all, how could he tell her that his heart had started beating when he'd met her? That she was the other half of his soul and in her eyes, he saw his future, the man he wanted to be. For her.

He pressed harder and bit gently at her nipple as his hand tugged at her other turgid tip until she cried out his name as she shattered beneath him. Peace overwhelmed him. It was as if her pleasure boomeranged back to him, in an all-encompassing circle. He moved up and cradled her in his arms. Kissing her tears away.

"I've got you."

"Always?" Her voice was faint.

"Always," he promised.

THE RINGING of his phone jarred him awake. He grabbed it off his nightstand.

"Hale," he answered.

"It's a go," Max Hogan said without preamble. "Get here now."

"Consider me on the road."

5

CAMILLA AND LISA HADN'T EVEN NEEDED TO TALK, THEY JUST looked at one another. When the kidnappers had demanded that everyone start walking, Lisa had taken the lead and Camilla stayed at the back of the pack. It didn't matter that they were surrounded by armed men; it gave Camilla a small sense of control, and she would take whatever she could get.

"Hurry up!" Raymundo demanded in Spanish as he shoved his rifle into her ribs.

Camilla would have loved to, but Roxanne was on her last legs and Camilla was having a tough time going any faster with the girl leaning on her.

"What did he say?" Roxanne wanted to know.

"I don't speak Spanish," Camilla answered.

"He said to move your ass," El Jefe answered in English from the Jeep he was driving. He laughed. "Do you want a ride?"

"Yes," Roxanne nodded eagerly.

"What are you willing to trade for one?"

"Ignore him," Camilla told the girl.

"But—"

"You need to ignore him," Camilla said again.

"Don't be a spoilsport. If I give her a ride, maybe she'll give me a ride. What do you think, pretty girl, is it a trade?"

Roxanne whimpered and started to walk faster. Camilla shot the man a dark look. He laughed again.

"She'll change her tune in a couple more hours." He gunned the engine and drove up to the front of the rag-tag line of prisoners. Camilla narrowed her eyes as she watched him. She needed the bug spray in her backpack. She slapped at another mosquito and wanted to scream or cry.

Keep it together, Ross! Crying is for babies.

Camilla bit her lip and saw tear tracks on Roxanne's cheeks. She wanted to comfort the girl, but she was walking at a good clip at the moment, and Camilla didn't want to interrupt her flow.

A horn honking reverberated through the jungle and everybody stopped walking. Camilla could see El Jefe standing on top of the hood of his Jeep, then he raised his rifle and let off some shots. Roxanne whimpered and Camilla winced.

"We're going to camp here for the night," he said in English.

Camilla couldn't believe it. It wasn't even sundown and the man was going to let them rest. She hoped that this time they would be allowed to get their belongings. She really wanted to clean up, maybe change her clothes.

"Come here," El Jefe roared as he pointed at Jan Hines. Camilla couldn't see her expression, but both Lisa Garcia and her boyfriend Paul Jeffries moved in on either side of her.

"What do you want with her?" Lisa demanded to know.

"Stay out of this if you want to stay alive," the boss said in Spanish. "It's time to start the ransom demands."

When Jan clung to Paul, El Jefe tilted his chin at one of his men and he meandered over and elbowed Paul in his neck. The young man dropped to the ground. Jan and a couple of the other girls shrieked. Lisa made a lunge toward the kidnapper as he grabbed Jan's elbows and jerked them behind her back. She cried out in pain.

"Stop it! Don't hurt her," Lisa yelled.

"Bitch, I told you not to interfere," El Jefe hollered in Spanish. "Don't force me to make an example of you to all of these Americans. I'll do it, but it'll be a waste."

"You don't have to hurt her," Lisa tried to argue reasonably.

"Don't cross me." The big man glared at her. His minion brought Jan to El Jefe, who hauled her up onto the hood of the Jeep. He made her kneel down in front of him.

"Which rich bitch are you?" he demanded to know. He was holding a handful of passports.

"Jan. I'm Jan," she stuttered.

He rolled his eyes. "What is your last name?"

Jan didn't say anything as tears started rolling down her face. Camilla wanted to rush up to the Jeep and grab her into her arms. Lisa walked to the Jeep and El Jefe gave her a fierce look.

"You're pushing your luck," he spit out in Spanish.

"You're scaring her so badly, she can't even remember her own name. You need my help."

"Fine. Make her talk."

"Let her down from there," Lisa said. Camilla wanted to cheer for the woman. At the same time, she wanted to yell at her for putting herself in danger like that.

Two men rushed Lisa and threw her up on the hood.

Camilla saw the makeshift bandage on her arm that was soaked through with blood and she winced, but Lisa didn't even flinch. El Jefe grabbed her by her hair. "What did you want to say to me?" he demanded in English. He wanted to terrify everyone and he was doing a damned good job.

"You're scaring Jan so badly that she can't think. Let me question her and I can get you the information you need."

El Jefe considered her. "Fine." He continued to keep his fist in Lisa's hair. Even with that, Lisa put one of her arms around Jan.

"Tell him your last name, Honey." Lisa coaxed.

"Hines, my last name is Hines."

El Jefe thumbed through the passports until he found hers. Then he put the rest in one of his cargo pants pockets. He pulled out a phone. Camilla had seen one of those before—a satellite phone. He shoved it at Jan.

"Call your parents."

She tried to hold the phone but she dropped it. It clattered to the hood, then fell to the dirt. One of the men picked it up and handed it back to her.

"Don't be stupid. Hold onto it this time and call your parents." El Jefe said in a mean whisper. Jan trembled as she pressed in numbers. El Jefe snatched the phone from her when she was done and put it on speaker.

"You have reached Covington Dry Cleaners, our hours of operations are—"

El Jefe's fist hit the back of Jan's head and she slumped down onto the hood, then her body slipped down onto the dirt of the jungle floor.

Lisa, free from El Jefe's grip, scrabbled off the hood and got on her knees next to Jan, resting her head in her lap.

"That's a minor punishment. The next person who lies to me will get cut." He looked around at the rag-tag group and pointed at Phyllis Agar, who was standing in front of Roxanne.

"You! Get over here."

Camilla stepped around Roxanne and put her arm around Phyllis.

"Let's go," she coaxed. She felt the girl trembling, so Camilla had to pull her along to the front of the crowd. When they got to the Jeep, Phyllis couldn't take her eyes off Jan who was crying in Lisa's arms.

El Jefe held his hand out to Phyllis, and once again Camilla coaxed the young woman. "Take his hand."

Phyllis turned pleading eyes at Camilla. "You need to do this," Camilla responded calmly.

Phillis took the man's hand and he hefted her onto the hood.

Camilla thrust out her hand. "Let me up," she demanded.

El Jefe glowered down at her.

"She's scared out of her mind," Camilla pleaded. "She's going to be of no use to you, let me help."

This time the man gave her a considering look and grunted. He held out his big hand and Camilla took it gratefully. She clambered aboard the Jeep and Phyllis practically fell into her arms. El Jefe shoved the satellite phone at Phyllis.

"Call your parents."

"Which one?" Phyllis asked.

That stumped the man for a moment. "Your father, he's rich, right?"

Phyllis looked up at Camilla for direction.

"Honey, who will pay a ransom for you?"

"They both will."

El Jefe let out a laugh. "I get more money." He looked out

into the crowd. "Two ransoms for the price of one," he yelled out. He grabbed Phyllis' hand and slapped the phone into it. "Call your father."

Again, she looked to Camilla for direction. "He's at work. I don't know his work number, it's programmed into my phone. I think I know his mobile number by heart."

"Call it!" El Jefe yelled at her.

Phyllis' fingers trembled as she pressed in the numbers. Before it had a chance to ring, the big man grabbed it and put it on speaker.

"Who is this?" A man's voice answered the phone angrily. Phyllis' whole face seemed to crumple as she started to cry.

"Answer him," El Jefe growled at Phyllis.

Camilla nudged Phyllis. "Say something, Phyllis."

"Phylly, is that you?" Her dad's voice changed, he suddenly sounded scared and anxious.

"Daddy? It's awful," she gasped out between sobs.

"Tell me where you are and I'll come and get you."

"It's not going to be that easy." El Jefe laughed. "Talk to your daddy, tell him everything the bad man has done. Tell him everybody I've killed."

Phyllis sobbed harder.

"Phylly, has he hurt you?" her father shouted.

El Jefe pulled out his knife. "Talk to your father," he said as he let the knife play with the hem of her fluttery top.

"Talk, Phyllis," Camilla used her school teacher voice.

"Talk!" El Jefe roared.

Phyllis jumped and the knife pierced her side. "Ahhh," she screeched.

"Phylly, what happened? Are you all right?"

"Daddy, he wants money. I'm afraid. Please pay him so I can come home. Please."

She sagged against Camilla who couldn't hold her upright. They both ended up in a heap on the hood of the Jeep.

"Did you hear that, Daddy?" El Jefe sing-songed. "Get as much money as you can ready, otherwise your daughter is going to die a horrible death at the hands of my men. I'll let them have fun with her first."

"Keep your fucking hands off my daughter! I'll get you your damned money."

"You have forty-eight hours. I'll give you the wiring instructions then."

El Jefe severed the connection and turned to Camilla. "Now it's your turn."

OF COURSE, Asher was leading the way, didn't matter if they were jumping into the desert, the water, or the jungle, somehow he was always the first man out of the plane. It always pissed off Cullen Lyons. The third time Nic looked over at Zed, the man rolled his eyes at him.

"I'm fine," Zed yelled over the roar of the plane engines. "Have a doctor's certificate to prove it and everything. If I didn't know better, I would say you were a parent."

Nic stiffened. He didn't want anyone to accuse him of having mothering instincts; that would blow his entire cover. Ezio laughed.

Before more laughter could ensue, Max shouted out. "Formation."

Everybody got in line behind Asher. Drone images had found the tour bus off the major highway. It was on its side. They still didn't have a list of passengers, but Nic's spidey senses were going off the charts. It was like he was channeling Zed. It had to be because it was Cami's alma mater.

Head in the game, Hale. Head in the game.

Nic closed his eyes for a second, then opened them. He watched as Asher jumped, then Cullen. He was the fifth man out of the plane. Nothing but green below; he was going to end up a tree for sure. Nic grinned. Asher and Cullen be damned, he lived for this shit too. He loved the float—it was serene, and for just a second Nic saw a hint of silver.

The bus!

He pulled his cord, trying to maneuver in that direction, but the wind was against him. He pulled harder and angled his feet. As he got closer to the ground he found himself moving to the north. Not close, but at least in the right direction.

Nic changed position, arrowing his feet and legs downward so he was less of a target to the tree limbs.

Nothing but leaves, baby. Nothing but leaves, he prayed.

Nic thumped onto the loamy jungle floor, his parachute tangled low in the trees above him. His grin damned near split his face as he gave a fist pump. He released the parachute and pulled, but it was no use, the thing was stuck.

"Who needs help, before I head for the bus?" he asked into his mic. Nic pulled out his handheld mini comp and pulled up his coordinates and where the bus was. One and a half klicks. Not bad.

"I have a visual on the bus," Zed said. "Just have to cut down."

"I'm at the bus," Max said. "Need help, Zaragoza?"

"No, I'm good."

"I see you, Ezio. Coming your way," Leo said.

Nic heard Raiden give a soft chuckle. "Asher, looks like you're in quite the predicament."

"Fuck off, Sato." Asher sounded off to the soft-spoken medic. Raiden laughed louder.

"What's so funny?" Kane asked.

"He's tangled in his parachute cord," Raiden said. "He's cutting his way out, but I'm loving how his leg is higher than his head."

"Enough. All of you get to the bus. This is not good."

A shiver ran down Nic's spine.

6

"YOU'VE GOT TO LET SOME OF THE GIRLS RIDE IN THE JEEP," Camilla begged for the umpteenth time.

Let me *ride in the jeep.*

She gritted her teeth so she wouldn't cry.

They had stopped for a brief respite so the soldiers could eat. They gave Camilla and the rest of the prisoners some food from their backpacks and some of the water from the jugs that they had on the Jeeps. It wasn't enough for everyone to keep up their energy for the miles that they'd been walking. For the first time in her life, she really wanted something good for herself, not a Ding Dong. It had just made her crash hard.

"What is she complaining about now?" El Jefe yelled in Spanish from the front Jeep.

"Same thing as the last time, she wants some of the bitches to ride in the Jeeps with us. But she's right, they're slowing us down."

"Are you telling me how to run this operation Marco?"

Marco held up his hands and shook his head. "No. Whatever you think is best, you know I trust you."

El Jefe gave a satisfied grunt. He pointed his finger at Camilla. "Come here."

Camilla walked slowly over to the big man who was grinning at her. "Your father hasn't called back. Why is that? Doesn't he love you?"

"He's probably out of the country. He works overseas a lot," Camilla said. It was the truth.

"Then you need to come up here and call your Mama."

Camilla broke into a cold sweat, praying that her mom wouldn't answer the phone. He reached down with his meaty paw. It was dirty, his fingernails were black. He must have seen her cringe because he laughed again.

"Poor princess, she doesn't like having to live in the real world. Get your ass up here." Camilla gave him her hand and he swung her up like she weighed nothing. She landed on her knees with a thud onto the hood.

"Isn't this a pretty picture?" He roared with laughter in Spanish. His men and Maria clapped. Camilla pushed herself into a standing position, jutted out her chin, and forced herself to look in El Jefe's face.

"Oh look, she's all brave."

More laughter.

He grabbed her chin and jerked it sideways, then he jerked it back the other way. "Not bad. If her parents don't pay, we can make some money if we sell her."

Don't listen. Don't listen. Think of something good. Something precious. Hazel eyes staring down at her, as his hand stroked down her belly—

"Listen to me!"

Camilla lurched over as he punched her stomach with the satellite phone. "Make the goddamn call."

She fumbled with the phone and caught it before it hit

the hood. Gasping for air, she looked up at El Jefe, trying to make sense of what he was saying.

"—better hope your mother answers the phone since your daddy didn't call back."

Camilla bit back a sob and then sucked in another deep breath.

"Use the phone, bitch."

It was hopeless, she had to make the call. With trembling fingers, she dialed. It barely had a chance to ring and she heard her mother's voice.

"Camilla?" She'd never heard her mother sound so upset, so utterly frantic.

"Camilla, is it you?"

"Mother—"

El Jefe yanked the phone out of her hand and shoved her off the Jeep. She grabbed at the top of the vehicle, trying to stop her fall. But her efforts just swung her around so that her chest hit the hubcap. The bolts bit in deep as her head hit the hard rubber tire before bouncing off the ground.

"Owww," she cried out. Her mouth tasted like dirt and copper.

"Just tell me what you want," her mother was saying.

"What is your daughter worth to you?" El Jefe chuckled.

"Let me talk to her."

Camilla rolled onto her back. Looking up she could see the canopy of trees and a small swatch of angry gray clouds. She grunted as the phone hit her belly in the same spot as last time.

"Talk to your mommy, *chiquita*."

Her arms didn't seem able to move, her hands felt like lead. Camilla rolled to her side, letting the phone slide to the ground.

"Camilla," she heard her mother say through the speaker. "Talk to me."

She pushed herself up so she was leaning against the wheel. Was her shoulder broken? She couldn't move her right arm. She picked the phone up with her left hand and dropped it in her lap.

"Mother," she lisped. Blood drooled down her chin.

"Is that you Camilla?"

"Yeth, ith me."

Don't cry. Crying never helps anything.

"What's happening? Tell me what precisely is going on. I want exact details."

When Camilla laughed, she coughed blood. Yep, her mother was still the same uptight physics professor.

She spat on the ground so she could speak clearly. "Precisely, I'm inth the Mexican jungle, with a bunch of students. We've beenth kidnapped. Some of the students have died. You need to tell this man you can raise at least a million dollars, otherwise, I will end up worse than dead, do you understand me?"

Thank God he had let Camilla talk to her mother to prep her. Her mother might be an unfeeling robot, but she was smart. She knew how to read between the lines of any situation.

"How do I get them the money?" Enid Ross finally asked.

Camilla flinched as El Jefe landed beside her. Once again he yanked the phone out of her hands.

"Hello, Mommy. In two days I will give you wiring instructions. You better answer the phone. Your daughter was telling the truth; there are things worse than death."

"I understand."

He broke the connection and shoved the phone into one of the many pockets on his cargo pants.

"Who else wants to ask for special consideration?" El Jefe yelled out to the students. Nobody said a word. He gripped Camilla beneath her armpits and jerked her into a standing position. She screamed in pain.

"Ahhh, poor girl, do you hurt?"

Camilla refused to answer. He pressed down on her injured shoulder and she screamed again.

"Answer me, do you hurt?"

"Yes," she bit out. At least the blood seemed to have stopped.

"That's good. Maybe you'll remember who is in charge."

He looked up, scanned the crowd of students, and pointed. "You, come here."

Camilla looked up and saw Travis Driver jogging toward her. He looked anguished. "Yes, sir?"

"Make sure she can keep up." He shoved Camilla into Travis' arms.

SHIT. Three shot and two dead due to injuries from the bus crash. No identification. By the looks of the clothes, one looked to be one of the kidnappers. The other four were American students who were in the bus. The dead kidnapper was already missing some body parts, likely due to a jaguar since he'd been outside of the bus.

"Par for the course, the kidnappers gathered all of their belongings so they could figure out who they had and make ransom demands," Kane said.

"Any luck on a passenger manifest?" Nic asked. He thought about some of the younger kids he knew before graduating who might have gone to William and Mary College. Were they on this bus?

Kane looked down at his tablet. "Not yet. The ETA is an hour. Not that it really matters, we just need to get to them before any more end up dead."

"Wrong," Max inserted. "If we could get the backgrounds of some of these kids, maybe we could find out if some of them have any hope of helping themselves or helping us. So far, the only one who seemed to be on their game was the tour guide."

"Point taken," Kane nodded.

Nic still wanted to know who was on the bus. He didn't recognize the two women or the one man who was shot in the chest. The second man, there was no hope of recognizing him, since half of his head was missing.

"What's wrong?" Raiden asked as he sidled up to Nic.

Nic stared at the girl at the back of the bus, her neck clearly broken.

"She looks so young."

Raiden sighed. "She's a baby. After what we've seen and done, I can't ever remember being so young."

"I know. Even when I *was* that young, I felt older."

"We've got to go," Raiden said as he motioned with his chin.

Nic nodded.

They stepped easily along the sides of the bus seats and hoisted themselves up and out of the bus door. They closed it up tight behind them. Kane and Leo were almost done burying the remains of the kidnapper. They didn't need his carcass attracting more predators to the other bodies in the bus.

"The Mexican authorities should be here in two or three days to recover the bodies," Max told the team. "The first two ransom demands have been made. Not surprisingly it was two of the girls. According to the manifest, there were fourteen passengers, as well as the bus driver and the tour guide."

"Do we have names?" Nic asked.

Max gave him an odd look, then answered. "Just the two who've called their parents. Their names are Phyllis Agar and Camilla Ross."

Time stood still and Nic went icy cold in the middle of the hot jungle. His vision narrowed so that he could only see Max. He couldn't hear anything, just watch as his Lieutenant's mouth moved.

He swayed and someone grabbed him.

"What the fuck, Hale? I hit you in the shoulder and you're down for the count? Did you get injured on the jump?" Cullen demanded to know.

"Huh?"

"Are you okay?" Cullen waved his hands in front of Nic's face as he spoke slowly and loudly.

"We lost him. It was bound to happen eventually. All those women finally drained him of his manly fluids and he's of no use."

Nic's fist shot out and glanced off Cullen's jaw. If the man hadn't stepped backward in time, he'd be down for the count.

Max twirled Nic around and grabbed both of his shoulders. "Hale! Look at me. What the fuck is going on?" he roared.

Nic shook his head, trying to clear it, trying to focus on his boss. "What were those two names again?"

"Ross and Agar," Max clipped out. "Which one do you know?"

"Camilla Ross, sir." Nic's voice was just as unemotional as Max's.

"Is this going to be a problem?"

Nic swallowed.

"Fuck. It's going to be a problem," Max growled. He looked over at his second in command. Kane immediately came over. "Watch him."

"It's not going to be a problem. I can do my job," Nic said. He kept his voice level and unemotional, but inside, his mind was swirling. How was it fucking possible that Cami was out here in this jungle? He jerked his head back to the bus, thinking of the young girl with the broken neck.

"Kane, you and Nic are twins on this job. Got it?"

Kane nodded.

Nic jerked his head in his boss' direction. Kane grabbed his arm. "We'll take the rear," Kane said to Max.

Max studied them both for a moment, then nodded.

Zed came up to Max. "I followed the tracks for a bit. Looks like three Jeeps. I counted eight sets of distinct footprints that weren't combat boots walking in between the vehicles. Three men, five women. There could be more."

"There are more," Kane said as he looked up from his tablet. "There were fourteen passengers on the bus, all from universities and colleges on the east coast. With four dead on the bus, they're down to ten, plus the tour guide."

"Kane, what else you got?" Max asked as the others gathered around.

"Camilla Ross is supposed to be some kind of teacher or leader on this expedition. The rest are mostly undergrads. Some of them come from really wealthy families, the bios are coming in slowly."

"What's the four-one-one on the tour guide, do we have anything more on her?" Max asked.

"She's led wilderness tours in Alaska, Montana, and Wyoming. She just started doing tours down here in Mexico this year. It's strange because they don't pay as well."

"Are you thinking she's in on it?" Asher asked.

Kane shrugged.

"Doesn't make sense if she's the one who made the S.O.S. call. I say we look at her as a friendly who can actually be of use," Max said grimly. He turned to Nic. "What about Camilla, she's a teacher. Does she have any skills that would help?"

"Last time I saw her was six years ago. I don't know."

"Okay." Max nodded. "Zed, you take point. Everyone else spread out. These tracks are too easy to follow; I want everyone on alert to make sure there are no booby-traps, or any unfriendlies left behind." Everyone gave Max an answer in the affirmative.

7

"Tell me about her," Kane coaxed. Or was he demanding? Nic couldn't tell, nor did he care, he just kept jogging forward. Forward, they needed to move forward. Fast. They needed to go faster.

"Nic. We'll get there, man. We're going to do this. But we've got to do it right. You've got to trust our team, the men up front. You can't get ahead of them."

Why is Zed on point? Godammit, I should be on point!

"Nic, slow down, you're getting ahead of the others. You know our position."

Nic didn't answer.

"Sailor!"

He turned his head. Kane was stone-faced, which was never good. He stopped in his tracks. Fuck, the man was right. He needed to get his head in the game. But...

Cami!

They were to the right of the barely-there road that the Jeeps had used to traverse through the jungle. Just in case someone was on that trail, they wanted to be out of sight.

"Nic, you gotta talk to me," Kane cajoled. "Who is

Camilla Ross to you? You said you haven't seen her for six years, man. She's practically a stranger now, right?"

He adjusted his rifle, making sure that it was secure and that he was ready for anything. He felt Kane's eyes on him.

"Once she was everything," he finally spit out. "Once she was my other half." Nic figured his voice was so low that Kane couldn't hear him above the cacophony of birds and monkeys and other jungle noises. He was wrong.

"But you were kids, right?" Kane's voice was soft too.

"Does that really matter?" Nic refused to look at his teammate.

They continued on for long minutes.

"No, it doesn't matter," Kane finally answered. "With A.J. it could be decades and I would still be there."

"Six years is damn near a decade," Nic spit out. "We've changed. There have been others. I don't know how she feels."

"I always knew your horn dog persona was bullshit."

Nic's head turned so fast it was amazing he didn't give himself whiplash. "What are you talking about?"

"Nic Hale, man whore. Nope, doesn't compute."

Nic was seriously confused. "How do you see that?"

"You were all talk, but I can count on one hand the times that I saw you go pick up a woman at the bar. Yeah, the women who were interested in having a SEAL on their scorecard definitely came onto you and all the rest of us, but I never saw you leave with any of them, no matter how hard they tried. But the next day you'd be all braggadocios. Nope, didn't compute at all."

Thank God for the camouflage paint; otherwise, Kane could have seen the flush turning his face red. Yep, he sure screwed the pooch on that.

How many other teammates did I fail to con?

"So, back to my original question. Tell me about Camilla."

"She was too good for me, that's who she was. I wanted to marry her, but we were too young. I met her when she was sixteen and a half and I was seventeen. We were the quintessential high school sweethearts, if you can believe that."

"What else?"

Kane kept his gaze forward, not missing anything. Nic forced himself to do the same, excising all visual memories of Cami from his brain so he could concentrate on the here and now.

"I already knew that I was going to join the Navy as an enlisted man. Follow in Dad's footsteps. I wanted to be a SEAL, learn things from the ground up before I applied to be an officer."

"Like we all don't know that," Kane smirked.

Nic went to adjust his rifle again, then stopped. It was a habit he had when he was uncomfortable, and a damn stupid one to have on a mission.

Keep it together.

"So how did joining the Navy pertain to you and Camilla?"

Nic climbed over a dead tree trunk, using a vine for support. "It was the one and only thing her parents and I ever agreed on—Cami needed to go to college, not become a Navy wife, following me around to each assignment."

"You knew you were going to be in Coronado or Little Creek, what was the problem? She could have attended college there."

"She was being scouted by schools like Yale, Harvard, and MIT. Full rides. I couldn't get in the way of that. She was adamant that she could go to a school in Virginia or California, but it wasn't the same thing."

"That's bullshit."

"You don't understand. She was – no, scratch that. She is brilliant. She planned to get a degree in Pure Mathematics."

"Are you shitting me? I work with some of the best programmers on the planet and hardly any of them get that degree."

"Her mother has a Ph.D. in Physics, her dad has a Ph.D. in Archaeology. She comes by it naturally."

They stopped as they saw Ezio hold up his fist ahead of them.

"Got something," Zed whispered through their receivers.

They all waited to see what Zed would say next. "This is where they camped. I have a body. It's not one of the students."

"Anything else?" Max whispered the question.

"Negative."

"Proceed with caution. We don't know if they left any surprises," Max said. "Kane, has there been any info that's come in yet about who we're dealing with?"

"Negative," Kane answered.

Kane was plugged into so many receivers, it was amazing that he had the bandwidth to question him, Nic thought as he rounded another stump. Seriously, that man was the king of multi-tasking.

A minute later they came upon the muddy clearing that marked where the group had camped for the night. The Jeeps had cut across through the light foliage into the clearing and then circled the area. It was clear that people had slept in the dirt.

"Found a Ding Dong wrapper," Leo called out.

"I got me an empty snack pack size of Doritos." Asher held up his prize.

"Obviously, we're not dealing with Boy Scouts, because nobody taught them how to police their area when they left," Cullen said. He was trying for humor, but it fell flat.

Ding Dongs. How many times had he watched Cami bite into one of those tasty chocolate cakes and sigh with bliss?

"Zed," Nic called out. "Is this from last night?"

He shook his head. "Night before last. We've got to get a move on."

"First, I want a better headcount of what we're dealing with," Max ordered. "Anybody who fucked up the tracks near the Jeeps answers to me."

Nobody rolled their eyes, but it was clear that the entire Night Storm team felt like doing it. They all knew the drill. Raiden took one Jeep, Asher another, and Leo the third. Meanwhile, Zed tried to determine just how many distinct prisoners there were.

It took forever for the team to come up with answers as far as Nic was concerned.

"I'm pretty sure there are three on this Jeep," Raiden said.

"We've got two on this Jeep, and one of them is tiny or it's a woman," Leo yelled out.

"I've got four on this one," Asher shouted.

Everyone waited to hear what Zed had to say. "I'm pretty sure that eleven people bedded down within this small perimeter here," Zed said. He indicated a small space that was circled by the three Jeeps.

"That would mesh with the fifteen people, minus the four dead from the bus."

Nic felt his entire body tremble. *Thank you, God.*

"Let's move out," Max commanded. "We're burning daylight."

———

EVERY STEP WAS AGONY. Fire raced through her body, and Camilla couldn't even see the person in front of her.

"We've got to stop, Doctor Ross."

"No, Travis," she gasped out. "Have to keep going." Camilla shook her head so she could actually see. She gave a little shriek when she did it, as another bolt of agony hit her hard. Travis stopped moving. and so did she. She had no choice since he was practically carrying her along beside him. They were bringing up the rear.

"I don't think your shoulder's broken. I think it's dislocated. I know how to fix it."

"We can't stop." Camilla tried to start walking on her own.

One step. Two steps.

I can do this. I've got this.

Three steps.

"Ahhhh." She tried to muffle her scream.

Pain like she never imagined flowed through her body. She'd hit her forehead, landed on her breasts, and jarred her shoulder, all spots injured from her time with El Jefe at the Jeep.

Travis rolled her over.

"Doctor Ross?" Travis' voice was filled with tears. "I shouldn't have let you try to walk. I'm so sorry."

Camilla bit her lip so that she wouldn't cry, but she tasted the salt of her tears. So much for that.

"Just lie there. I'm going to try to put your shoulder joint back into place."

"Don't," Camilla begged. "Just help me up."

"I've got to. It's the only way to help you. I've seen a lot of injuries on the football team. Your shoulder isn't broken, it's dislocated, trust me."

This was the last kid in the world she would trust. He placed one hand firmly on her sternum; she figured it was to keep her in place, but it fucking hurt. "Please lift your hand. I'll stay still," Camilla begged.

Travis looked down at her chest and he must have seen some of the bruising above her tank top because he yanked his hand away.

"Sorry, I didn't mean to hurt you more than I have to."

For the first time, he didn't seem arrogant; he seemed like an anxious kid who was trying to do something right. Camilla hoped he'd pull it together and be able to help her.

"Relax your arm as much as you can. Take some deep breaths. I know it's tough, but you're tough, you can do it."

Camilla snorted and snot came out her nose. Really? He was doing guided meditation? She thought she heard an engine getting close, but she ignored it and tried to relax.

Travis gently moved her arm so that it was parallel to her body, then he bent it at the elbow and twisted her forearm so that her palm was facing up.

Camilla was sure that her breathing technique was the same as a woman would use if she were in labor.

"Get up!" a man yelled.

Travis gripped her elbow and forearm. His hands were surprisingly gentle and he guided them over her head. Camilla shut her eyes and saw red behind her lids.

"Ahhhhhhhh."

Her world went black.

She felt something prodding her ribs.

"Get up! You need to start walking!"

"She needs a doctor," Travis cried out.

"All of you Americans are soft."

It was a boot. The man was kicking her ribs with the toe of her boot, but the pain was nothing compared with the pain in her shoulder and her breasts.

"He's right." El Jefe bellowed in Spanish. The kicking stopped. "Some of the women are slowing us down too much."

Camilla opened her eyes. Now El Jefe and the kicker were standing over her, with Travis between them.

"You," El Jefe said in English as he motioned to Travis, "pick her up and put her in the Jeep."

"She needs medical attention," Travis pleaded.

"If you care so much, take care of her. Take care of all the whiny women. We have a schedule to meet," El Jefe waved his hand at Travis, dismissing him.

Camilla groaned as Travis picked her up. Being moved was agony, but at least now she and the other injured were going to get some relief. The girls needed to be able to stop walking, otherwise, they'd drop in their tracks.

"What are you doing?" Camilla heard Maria ask in Spanish. "You're babying her," she complained.

Camilla turned her head to watch the byplay between the two of them as Travis walked slowly toward a Jeep.

"Maria, you know we need to meet the trucks and get to the village."

"Leon, you're always a soft touch. These women need to toughen up. They're going to be with us for a while. This is nothing compared to what's coming next." Maria shook her head in disgust.

"I know mi corazón, but we need internet access to get to the bank accounts."

"But—"

"Enough! I'm in charge."

Camilla saw Maria wince. She would have liked to see El Jefe backhand the woman like he was prone to do, but no such luck. Of course, she would probably just get up and hit him back.

"No! Don't lay her down, she sits. There's not enough room for her to lie down in the Jeep." It was the kicker talking. Camilla was dizzy and she felt like she was going to throw up. She found herself in the backseat of a dirty Jeep, then Jan was sitting next to her. The girl wasn't even conscious; how had she been walking?

Jan sank forward and then started sliding off the seat. Camilla made a grab for her with her left hand, but Paul was there before Camilla could get a good hold.

"I've got her," he said. Gently, he propped her into the seat and did up her seatbelt.

"Doctor Ross, you need to put on your seatbelt too," Travis said.

Hell, I'd forgotten all about the kid.

Camilla turned to look at him and immediately regretted it as the pain sliced through her neck. "Thanks for your help," she gasped out.

"Are you okay?"

"I'm fine," she said. She blinked back tears.

Camilla struggled with the seatbelt and hissed in a breath when it tightened across her breasts. The pain...

The driver swung into his seat then glared at Travis and Paul. "Get back in line, we're moving out.

The Jeep rumbled to life, and with the first up and down thrust over the non-existent road the seatbelt bit into her breasts and she moaned. She tried to stay conscious. Tried to think of anything good in her life. Any good memory that would get her through this hell.

. . .

CAMILLA LOOKED up at Nic in frustration. How could he not budge on this issue? It made no sense.

"I should never have told you about those scholarships."

"Yes, you should have. We agreed to always be honest with one another, remember?"

"Admit it; before I told you about MIT and Harvard, you were considering marrying me before you joined the Navy."

He didn't meet her eyes.

She was cuddled on his lap in his small apartment. She reached up and cupped his cheek, turning his face so he was forced to look at her.

"You were going to ask me to marry you, weren't you?"

His hazel eyes darkened. He nodded.

"Baby, I've got it figured out. Marry me, and ask to be stationed in Virginia. I have a full ride waiting for me at William and Mary College. It's only an hour away from Little Creek, Virginia. We can make this work."

"And what about if I'm assigned to Coronado?" he asked.

"That makes it even easier, I go to San Diego State University. This is doable."

She watched as he hesitated. It was time for the big guns. Camilla started to unbutton the front of her sundress. Where before Nic's eyes had darkened, now they shot sparks of gold as he watched her undo each button—past her bra, past her waist, past her panties, until it was wide open.

He sucked in his breath.

Camilla didn't have to wait long for his hand to cover her stomach, he felt so hot. His other hand tangled in her hair and he bent down to kiss her. A mere brush of his lips against hers, a tantalizing taste as his breath wafted across her lips. He smelled like mint. He came back and brushed his lips against hers again, this time with a little more force, and she moved her face, trying to prolong their kiss, but he moved too quickly.

The third time he went to tease her, she grabbed his head and sifted his shaggy hair through her fingers. She bit into his scalp with her nails, anything to keep his lips on hers so that she could have his mouth the way she wanted it. She needed him, his taste, his breath. She could feel his smile as he parted his lips against hers and she flowered open, taking his tongue inside her mouth, moaning in appreciation.

His strong fingers massaged her scalp. It felt so good, but not as good as the spicy taste of Nic Hale as he stroked his tongue against hers. She could have wept with relief at the beauty of this kiss. She sucked on his tongue, and he moved back and nipped at her bottom lip and gave a small tug. Camilla felt her body start to go liquid at the evocative caress. She needed him to move his hand.

"Please, Nic."

He looked down at her, his eyes searching. That was when she remembered he was as new to this as she was. She wondered if he was as prepared for tonight as she was.

"Tell me what you need, Cami, and it's yours."

"I need my bra off, and your shirt off." She struggled to sit up so she could get out of her dress, and then unsnap her bra.

He pulled her close and easily smoothed the dress down her arms, lifting her slightly so that it fell to the floor. Camilla shivered, in a good way.

"Is this what you wanted?" he asked. His voice was deeper, smokier.

"My bra," she whispered.

He was looking down at her body, his eyes intent. Did he like what he saw? She took a deep breath, sucking in her stomach.

"Don't do that," he said as he traced his fingers along the skin of her tummy. "Relax."

How could she relax? She was about to be naked in front of Nic for the very first time. It was scary and wonderful all at the same time.

"You know we can't go too far; I don't have—" he started.

"I have condoms in my purse," Camilla interrupted.

He froze. She'd surprised him. Good. She reached up, cupping his face, and leaned in for a kiss. When he didn't respond she pulled back.

"Are you sure?"

"I've never been more sure about anything. I want us to make love."

His big body shuddered. He pulled her closer for another one of his soul-shattering kisses. She had no idea how long they stayed like that, lost in each other's arms, but then he tugged her hand out of his hair and she felt her bra strap ease down her arm. He soon had her out of her bra and he tossed it to the floor.

She looked up at him, her eyes heavy with passion. When had he taken off his shirt? It didn't matter. She pushed her breasts against his hot chest, moaning at the lush sensation of skin against skin. Levering herself against his abdomen she pushed herself into a kneeling position. His hazel eyes watched her as she went to work on the buttons of his jeans.

"Hold on."

She looked up at him in confusion.

He sat up and pulled the throw blanket from off the back of the couch and wrapped it around her shoulders. "We're going to my bedroom." He pulled her close as they headed down the hall.

"My purse." she pointed.

He gave her a roguish look, then swept it up in his hand.

"Anything else?" he asked.

She shook her head.

He guided her towards his room. Her heart started beating

faster. Would she really be able to talk Nic into making love with her tonight?

Once the door was closed behind them, he pulled her in for a kiss. The blanket was in the way of her wrapping her arms around him, but it didn't matter, because his lips were on hers and it felt sublime. He took the kiss deeper; her thoughts whirled around her head until they all centered on being cocooned by Nic. His tongue thrust into her mouth and she tasted his want, his need, and most of all, his love.

For a moment she felt like she was flying, then Camilla found herself gently placed in the middle of Nic's bed. She smiled up at him, his hazel eyes, and that dimple in his chin. The blanket fell away and she could move her arms. She traced the cleft, then touched his lips. She read every concern in his eyes, his every worry. But he wanted, Lord how her man wanted.

"You have to be sure, Cami. Are you?" he whispered.

"You have to be sure too, Nic. I'm the one who wants to divest you of your virginity, are you ready for that?"

His eyes went wide and he threw back his head and laughed. He had the best laugh of anybody she knew.

He stood up by the side of the bed, undid the rest of the buttons on his jeans, and pulled them off along with his underwear. This time her eyes went wide.

"Divest away." His grin was devilish.

8

THREE HOURS OF SHUT-EYE HAD BEEN THREE HOURS TOO MANY as far as Nic was concerned. The good news was that Zed figured they were only about four hours behind the students.

"In two hours were going to come to a fork in a road, if you can call this a road." Kane pointed to the piss-poor drone image on his tablet. "Both ways end in villages, both with about the same size populations and both equally poor. It's a crapshoot which way they'll go."

"Is there anyone we could send out to each village?" Nic asked. It was a long shot, but he had to ask.

Max looked him dead in the eye and shook his head. "Sorry, Nic, I made the call all the way to your dad. Nobody could get here in time. It's all us or the local federales."

"Fuck them, we never know whose side they're on," Cullen bit out.

Most everybody on the team nodded. Unfortunately with the way the Mexican economy was going, more and more of the government was on the take.

Nic was sick of this shit. All he cared about was getting Cami home, safe and alive.

Once again Zed took point and Nic was in the rear. This time Raiden was his babysitter.

"You doing okay?" Raiden asked.

Nic sent him a sideways glare.

Raiden held up his hands. "Hey, didn't mean to suffer the wrath, just asking a question."

Nic settled, just a bit. Raiden was one of the coolest members of the team. He was the only one he had told about Alice and Mimi. Not the part about spending time with them when he said he was out chasing skirts, but he had told Raiden about helping his cousin out. He'd wanted advice. Yeah, Raiden was the best.

"I've been better," Nic answered. "I can't fucking believe that my Cami is one of the ones who has been kidnapped."

"Yours?" Raiden asked quietly.

"She was mine through junior and senior year of high school, then the summer we graduated. Years might have passed, but I guess in my heart she's always been mine. How fucked-up is that?"

"The heart wants what the heart wants."

"Is that some kind of quote?" Nic asked.

"I think it's Emily Dickinson, but I might have gotten it wrong. I figured I should quote her since we were talking about high school love."

"Raiden Sato, you're a pain in my ass," Nic said with a half-laugh.

"Got you laughing though." There was a glint in Raiden's black eyes. "So why aren't there little Camis and Nics running around right now?"

"There were supposed to be. Silly woman wanted to get married after we graduated, but I sure as hell wasn't on board with that. I knew how rough my first couple of years in were going to be. I didn't want to end up divorced. What's more, she's a bona fide genius, she had scholarships up the ass. Her parents both had or I should say, have Ph.Ds.. They wanted their princess to go to Ivy League, but then when she got the full ride to MIT, all bets were off. That's where they wanted her to go for her math degree."

Raiden whistled.

"Yeah, right? That's the woman who was so in love with me, that she wanted to drop everything and be a sailor's wife. Can you imagine?"

Raiden didn't respond for half a klick. "Yeah, I could imagine. How did you break it off with her?"

Nic snorted. "How do you manage to crawl into my head?"

"Practice. So how did you break it off? Were you sneaky or up front?"

"God, it was tough, but I was up front. I loved her. There wasn't a chance in hell I was going to be anything but truthful with her, she deserved my utmost respect. Of course, she totally blew me off. She was tighter than a tick," Nic laughed as he thought about how she was. She'd been magnificent.

"What?"

"Huh?"

"What are you laughing about?"

"Her. Always her. God, Raiden, Cami was a force to be reckoned with. First, there was her logic. That woman could out-argue a supreme court justice. She had it figured out that I was going to the SEALs, so I would be based in either Coronado, California or Little Creek, Virginia. So she started her campaign. California was easy because it was

San Diego State. That school was killer, and she had a full-ride offer. Virginia was trickier."

"How so?" Raiden asked.

"Camilla explained how close William and Mary College was, and how she could study there and get just as good an education as she would at Harvard, MIT, or anywhere else. Hell, she sent the curriculums and the professor bios to me through certified mail. Then when I still balked, she had one of the alumni of W&M show up at my apartment when she was there, forcing me to listen to him."

"She didn't."

"Oh yes, she did." Nic grinned, remembering how pissed-off he'd been. How impressed he'd been.

"What was she planning on majoring in?"

"Mathematics. There was this famous mathematician who was a professor at W&M that she intended to study under. She'd been offered a full ride at that school. Her parents were furious that she was even considering it. They were bound and determined that she go to MIT."

"How did you find that out?"

"Little girl might have been fighting her fight, but don't think that her parents weren't on my ass."

"How'd they get to you?"

"They didn't really, they went to my parents."

Raiden laughed and laughed some more. "Oh shit, I would have loved to have seen that. I haven't met your mother, but I've heard stories. And your father? Captain Hale doesn't take shit from anybody. I can't imagine him putting up with some interfering Ph.Ds.. What did they do?"

"I don't know. They told me about their visit, and how adamant the two Doctor Ross's were that I not marry their daughter. Apparently, a sailor wasn't good enough at any point. Mom was pissed."

"I imagine. Did you tell Cami?"

"Fuck no. Her campaign only would have intensified, then she would have been angry with her parents, and I would have hated that. But her parents solidified my stance. She needed to go to school and totally focus on that, not try to juggle a new marriage."

"So, I repeat my original question," Raiden said as they made their way through a particularly dense part of the jungle. "What did you do to convince her to wait?"

"I told her there wasn't a chance in hell we were getting married before I joined the Navy. I told her. She didn't believe me. Eventually, I told her to register for William and Mary College, because she had convinced me that was the right university for her undergraduate degree. She figured because of that, she had me. The day her first class began, I was off to Lake Michigan for my first day of training."

"So no wedding," Raiden sighed.

"Nope. Jesus, did my phone blow up. She even flew up to Chicago to the Great Lakes Naval Training Center."

Raiden laughed again.

"Hey, it wasn't funny," Nic glared at him.

Raiden raised his hands in surrender. "I'm just liking her more and more. She's going to need that kind of resilience right now. So tell me how all of this ended. Why didn't you just marry her after she graduated?"

Nic closed his eyes for a moment, then opened them to watch where he was going. He remembered following her college career at William and Mary, even though he was going through intensive training to become a SEAL, he kept tabs on her. In all that time he'd never once lifted the communication embargo, not wanting to derail her career, wanting her to stay focused. But when he got his trident, it had been time. It was the summer after her junior year. He'd sent her a letter. He knew that she'd be back with her parents. He didn't want to call her, instead he'd poured out his heart. He told her that he was stationed in Little Creek as a SEAL. He knew they could make this work. He loved her, and wanted to see her. He waited three weeks and there was no reply. He figured he deserved that. He'd been too much of a wuss to call her, what he needed to say needed to be said in person or in writing, so he kept sending letters, ten in all. It wasn't until September that he had gotten a response.

The return address was her parents, inside was nothing more than a newspaper clipping of an engagement announcement, Camilla Ann Ross and Harris Prescott.

"Nic, you still with me?"

"Not really," Nic admitted. "Don't we have a mission?"

"Seriously, what happened next?"

"It ended. End of story. We went our separate ways, and I followed the age-old sailor tradition of wine, women, and song."

He could feel Raiden looking at him, but he ignored him. All that mattered was the here and now. They had people to rescue. They had Cami to rescue.

And her last name was still Ross, not Redmond.

"Up!"

Camilla didn't know what was going on.

"I said get up. If you don't start listening, I'm going to just drag your sorry ass out of the Jeep."

Who is the woman yelling at me? Where's Nic?

"Ahhhhh," Camilla cried out when her hair was yanked as she was pulled sideways against her seatbelt.

"Finally, I have your attention. Get out of the Jeep. Even after we give you a ride, you find a way to slow us down."

Camilla heard sobbing. "Don't touch me. Please don't touch me."

She tried to turn her head and see what was happening in the seat next to her, but Maria was holding her hair too tightly.

"Let me unbuckle my seatbelt," Camilla said in her schoolteacher's voice. Anything to make Maria let her loose so she could help Jan.

Maria shoved her head away. "Be quick. We don't have all night." That was when Camilla realized it was dark. She also noticed a loud rumble that she hadn't heard before, but she didn't have time to look around. Instead, she unbuckled her belt and focused on Jan. There was some thug groping her. Quickly, she pushed the man's hands away, unbuckled Jan's seatbelt, and pulled her toward her side of the Jeep.

"Hey, what are you doing?" the man demanded in Spanish. Camilla ignored him. She stumbled out of the Jeep before finally getting upright. When she was firmly on her feet, she tugged Jan into her arms.

"Shhh, it's going to be all right," she comforted the girl.

"Why lie to her?" Maria laughed.

Jan shuddered against Camilla's throbbing shoulder. Were they ever going to get out of this?

"Time to get into the truck!" a man yelled. Headlights blinded Camilla for a moment.

"What's going on?" she asked Maria.

"You're always bitching about people needing to ride. Well, Princess, you'll be happy; now everybody gets to ride.

You and that sniveling bitch need to move your ass, we don't have all night. We need to get to the village by morning."

"What's going to h-h-happen to us?" Jan stuttered.

"If your parents pay, then you won't spend too long in your cage. Maybe just a month or so. It won't be so bad. Maybe your cage will be next to that pretty boy's who's always so protective of you, won't you like that?" Maria taunted.

The woman was trying to mind-fuck them, there was no other term for it. Camilla hated her more than she did El Jefe.

"Now move your asses onto the truck." She sauntered away, leaving them to fend for themselves.

Now that Camilla's eyes had adjusted she saw that there was a canvas-covered truck that looked like it had been built in the nineteen-fifties on the road in front of them. Most of the college students were climbing inside. Lisa wasn't; she was standing at the back bumper looking around, making sure everybody was getting onboard.

"Camilla!" she shouted out.

"I'm here," Camilla shouted back. "I have Jan with me. We're coming."

Camilla let out a sigh of relief when she saw Lisa head there way. Trying to keep Jan upright was using what little strength she had left. She realized that Lisa's arm had to be killing her, but hopefully, between the two of them, they could manage to get Jan onto the truck.

"Some of the guards hustled the guys onto the truck, that's why they're not here to help," Lisa said as soon as she was close.

Camilla nodded, she had wondered.

Between the two of them, they made quick work of

getting Jan to the truck. Travis and Paul were at the edge to help all three of them up when they got there.

"Where are we going?" Camilla asked Travis as she glanced over at the two stone-faced men with their rifles pointed at Paul and Brian.

"They said something about a village. All they keep talking about is the food. Sounds good to me."

Camilla nodded. Food would be good. She looked over at Lisa. She was looking as wan as she and Jan. Camilla needed to think of a way to get them some help.

"Once our parents pay up, everything will be all right, right?" Travis asked her quietly. She sat as straight as she could with her shoulder hurting as badly as it was. He needed her to be strong, she was in charge after all.

"Yes," she lied outright. She refused to think of what Maria had said. "They know the only way they will get their money is if they return all of you unharmed."

The eagerness in his eyes about broke her heart. "Really?"

"Absolutely," she confirmed.

"That's good. That's real good."

The truck hit a bump and she almost toppled onto her side. Her eyes smarted with tears. She bit her lip. She couldn't let herself cry, otherwise, she might not stop.

You can be strong, Camilla, she reminded herself.

I'm Camilla!

Remember who Dad named you after.

Camilla let out a snotty snort-laugh and wiped her nose with her sleeve. Yeah, here she was, Camilla Ross, named after the great Roman virgin warrior and she wasn't doing crap.

"Some warrior I am," she mumbled.

"What did you say? Are you okay?" Travis asked as he helped her back up into a sitting position.

"I'm fine. Go help Lisa," she said.

Think, Camilla, think. She hurt so bad and she knew a fever had started. Great—fuzzy brain, just what she needed.

Think.

She looked out the back of the truck. Rain. Perfect. At least they were in the truck, but God knew where they were taking them. What was next?

9

"WE'VE GOT A PROBLEM," NIC HEARD ZED SAY THROUGH HIS receiver. Raiden glanced over at him, having heard the same thing.

"What?" Max demanded to know.

Nic and Raiden sped up to meet up with all the others.

"We've got a fork in the road and the rain has doused all the tracks."

Nic's heart stopped. He and Raiden ran faster; their boots kept them steady on the wet and slippery jungle floor. When they met up with the group, everybody was there except Zed and Cullen, their two best trackers.

"Any word?" Nic managed to keep the anxiety out of his voice as he addressed his lieutenant.

Max shook his head.

Kane sidled up next to him. "We're going to get them, you know that, right?"

Nic gave one short nod.

He looked the group over. Nobody looked tired, everybody looked as fresh as the moment they had jumped out of the plane. He was probably the one who looked the most strung out if he had to guess.

Nic watched as Kane went over to Max and grabbed his tablet out of his pack. That damn thing could handle gale-force hurricane winds and rain, a little drizzle here in the jungle was nothing.

He watched the two of them put their heads together and talk over some things as Kane pointed to things on the tablet. Please God, say Kane knew something...anything.

"I got nothing," Zed said. Nic heard him in stereo as his voice came over his receiver and Zed came out from the road on the right. "The mud's too deep; it washed away whatever tracks might have been there."

Two minutes later, Cullen echoed Zed's words when he came back to the team. Max motioned for everyone to gather round.

"There are two villages along each fork in the road, if you can even call them that. They don't have names. We know about them through satellite photos that have scanned them in the past."

Everybody pressed to look at Kane's screen so they could see what in the hell he was talking about.

"That doesn't look like a village, that looks like three little houses," Ezio said.

"Yeah," Leo agreed. "Village my ass."

Kane looked up and glared at both men. "They're villages. Look at how much land has been cleared. From the satellite, we're lucky that we're seeing the three buildings. God knows how much more there is."

"I'm shutting up now," Leo said.

"Tell me more," Ezio demanded.

Nic was in Ezio's camp. "Where does the road go after the so-called village?"

"It takes about eight more hours before they finally get to Once de Mayo."

"That has to be their final destination, right? They need internet and a bank. They won't get it where there are just three damn houses," Nic asserted.

"Don't be so sure of that," Kane said slowly. "They could have quite the set-up in the middle of nowhere if they have someone who knows what they're doing."

"Okay, that's the left fork," Asher said. "What's behind door number two, the right fork?"

Kane tapped his tablet and showed another part of the jungle. "This is village number two, again there is no name. This time we have five buildings. It is on the way to Villa Hermosa."

"Zoom in further," Raiden demanded. Kane did. "It doesn't look like there is much of anything after that. At least with Once de Mayo, it takes them to a main highway eventually. Villa Hermosa just goes deeper into the jungle."

Nic had a bad feeling about that. "So the kidnappers go to the no-name village, then they move onto Villa Hermosa. Anywhere between there, they can hide the hostages until they get paid. The other way leaves them more exposed."

Everyone nodded in agreement.

"It's a crapshoot," Cullen spat out.

"You called it," Max agreed. "We're splitting up."

Before Max could assign anybody Nic threw out his preference. He didn't give two shits about protocol at this point. "I want the right."

Max gave him a cool assessment. "Nic, me, Raiden, Cullen, and Zed are on the right. The rest of you go with Kane to the left."

Nic perked up. Max was sending five to the right and four to the left. That meant he had the same kind of feeling he did. They better be damn well heading out at a fucking run.

"We need to shut this shit down," Max said. "We're going full out, got it?"

Everybody nodded, most of the men grinned.

"Let's move."

FOR ONCE CAMILLA was awake when a vehicle stopped. Not alert, but at least she was awake. Out of the back of the truck, the first thing she noticed were children. They were peeking out from small little homes, their eyes wide before they were hustled back inside.

"Out, all of you, out."

The tailgate was opened, and there stood El Jefe with his arms crossed. He was grinning like he had won the lottery.

"Let's see the merchandise."

One of the guards from the truck jumped out while the other one stayed on the truck to shove them out. Camilla was first.

"Ahh, the troublemaker." El Jefe said when she landed in front of him. "Wait until you see your new accommodations. You'll be pleased, I'm sure."

It was dusk. They were in the middle of a village by the looks of things. She saw one building that had a cross on it. The church. It was made of adobe bricks—how in the world had they gotten the clay?

Quit geeking out and look around.

Looking closer, one of the homes looked like it might be some kind of store, but she wasn't sure. One obvious thing was that now that everybody was in hiding, there was nobody on the street and all of the doors were closed. It was just the truck and the three Jeeps in the middle of the tiny little village square. Just El Jefe's people, Camilla, and all the rest.

Out of the corner of her eye, she saw something else.

What was that? Was that an antenna?

"Do you like what you see?" El Jefe asked.

Camilla jerked around to look at him. He was still smiling. It was then she noticed the long rope he was holding. "Give me your hands."

She heard the kids behind her getting out of the truck while she put out her hands. El Jefe tied the thin nylon rope around her wrists. She kept her wrists side to side so that there would be more give after he was done. Thank God she did considering how tight he tied the knot. Then he wrapped the rope around her waist.

"I think you should be next," he said. He was pointing to someone behind her. She turned to look, and El Jefe cuffed the back of her head. "Mind your own business."

It wasn't much of a hit. In fact, it was minor, all things considered. Who knew that she'd be rating the impact of blows four days ago? Camilla felt the tug of her rope as it was used to connect her with the person behind her.

"Ouch," she heard Roxanne cry out.

"I'll just tie it tighter if you don't stop whining."

The man got off scaring the hell out of everyone.

Camilla could hear the shuddering breaths that Roxanne was taking behind her.

Good girl, you're not sobbing.

"Ah, now we have our little hero. Hands behind your back. I don't need any shit from you." She assumed he was talking to Travis.

On and on it went, until finally, Camilla heard him talking to Lisa. She cringed when she heard Lisa cry out. If

Lisa made a sound, it must have been bad, whatever El Jefe did to her.

How was her arm?

Was it infected?

How about Jan?

Fingers snapped in front of her. She jerked her head upwards and pain shot through her shoulder. "Uppy, uppy, bitch. You need to stay awake, there's a lot of work that needs to be done."

Maria grabbed at the rope that was hanging down from Camilla's tied hands and yanked. As she moved forward, Roxanne knocked into her.

"I'm sorry," the girl said.

Maria laughed. "This is all part of the fun, seeing you all try to learn to walk together. You'll all fall on your asses and be dragging one another along. I love this."

She turned around and dropped the rope over her shoulder, then started marching toward the church. Camilla had to almost run to keep up. She felt a huge tug on the rope behind her, then she fell backward against Roxanne. Maria was standing over her, laughing.

"I told you how it would be. You can't keep up."

Camilla struggled to her feet and got a good look at everybody behind her. Nearly half of the students were on the ground—all of the girl students along with Travis. She watched as Brian Lane tried to help him up since Travis' hands were tied behind him. Lisa was still on her feet and she was helping Phyllis and Leslie to get up off the ground.

"Maria, you have ten minutes to get them strung up in front of the church, got it?" He yelled over at her in Spanish.

"Got it," she yelled back.

Then she yelled at two guards who were still at their Jeeps and told them to get over and help her. Camilla saw that a couple of the other men were pounding on the villagers' doors and displaying their guns. The women who answered looked just as terrified as Camilla felt. Wait a minute, were there more men than there had been?

She looked some more and saw another truck and two more Jeeps.

Jesus, God, what was going to happen to them?

One of the doors was wrested off its hinges and two guards stormed in.

"What are you looking at?" a guard demanded in English. Camilla's rope was yanked and she stumbled forward, but somehow managed to stay on her feet. Now the little village square was teeming with people. She saw more men in fatigues, and that new truck had some kind of antenna attached to it that looked like something on a news truck. So she *had* seen an antenna. What's more, there was a satellite dish.

"Food, lots of food." She heard someone shout behind her.

"Faster," Maria said as she yanked harder and walked faster. The rope bit into her wrists, but it would have been worse if she'd let them tie them as tightly as they'd wanted.

"Ahhh," she let out a scream as her arms were yanked forward and her waist was dragged backward. Roxanne had fallen again, pulling Camilla's shoulder out of the socket.

"Get moving!" Maria yanked harder.

Camilla shrieked, hating the sound that came out of her throat. The pain swirled around her body and then dripped over her head and shoulder like a lava flow. Her body was being ripped apart by the taut rope, her muscles beginning to stretch to the breaking point.

"You're worthless. Do I have to carry you?"

The words didn't make sense until she careened into Maria as the pull of the rope behind her let loose.

"Ah, fuck," Maria said. "We're never going to get this done. Jorge, come here."

Jorge picked Camilla up and she cried out again.

"Where's El Jefe?" Maria asked.

"In the truck. He's working to get the satellite internet up," a man responded.

"Take this knife," Maria said.

Even through her tears, Camilla saw the big knife flash in front of her. No matter how bad the pain was she didn't want to die. She struggled to get out of the guard's arms. He hugged her tighter. "I'm just cutting the rope," he growled.

She didn't get any kind of relief when her hands were cut free, the overall pain was too overwhelming. She tried to keep her eyes open, but she lost the battle.

RIGHT HAD BEEN the right way to go, but Jesus, what in the hell was going on? Max had the five of them spread out, so that they had the village surrounded, trying to get as much intel as possible. It had killed him to go past the prisoners to the back of the village where there were only a couple of dilapidated shacks, with no sign of life.

"I've got nothing," Nic reported in. "I think these two huts have been abandoned. I'm going to go further around, closer to Zed."

"Agreed," Max said over the mic. "I've contacted Kane, the others are on their way."

"Any ETA?" Cullen asked.

"Kane will report back in when he has one," Max answered.

Nic moved quietly through the jungle, staying deep in the foliage but close enough so he could see what was going on. The further he moved toward Zed, the closer he got to the back of the church and away from possibly spotting Cami.

"I count eleven," Raiden said. "All of them are hanging from their wrists off of some sort of scaffolding in front of the church."

"Motherfucker," Cullen's voice was harsh.

"At least their feet are touching the ground. Three of the women are hanging by just one arm. They're not in good shape," Raiden continued.

Nic's stomach rolled. He felt his gorge rise.

Keep it together.

"I've got a count. We've got twenty-three we need to take out, which includes one woman. If I had to guess, the guy in charge is sitting in the chair in front of the tied-up prisoners."

Nic listened to Zed's report. Twenty-three against five, that was...doable...with time and planning. Twenty-three against five with eleven hostages? That was going to be a problem.

"We've got a lot of incidental targets. Four women outside of their houses over cooking fires. Shit, man, some of them have kids with them. It's a fucking menagerie," Cullen reported.

It just kept getting worse and worse. Nic tasted vomit and spat on the ground.

"We're going to have to go in tonight," Max said. "Raiden, how bad are we talking? How are the prisoners holding up?"

"I'd say at least two broken bones and a head wound for sure," Raiden said slowly. "One is unconscious, but I don't see any contusions around her face, but with the way her arm is hanging down, she could just be out of it from pain. I don't see a choice but waiting until tonight."

"Agreed," Max said. "I want all of you monitoring this situation. It's two hours until sundown, I want to take them at zero three hundred. Any unfriendly who leaves the village to take a smoke or a piss after zero two hundred, you take him out quietly, understood?"

Everyone answered in the affirmative.

"In the meantime," Max continued, "I want you, Zed, to be scoping out the best goddamn tree that you can find for a sniper position. The rest of us will go in nice and quiet, Zed will start in when the ruckus starts."

Nic could hear Zed's grin over his receiver.

"I want to go across and see the prisoners," Nic said after everything was said and done.

His request was met by a moment of silence.

"Can you keep your head in the game?" Max asked.

"Absolutely. What's more, I can give you intel on Camilla Ross, describe what kind of asset she could be if that's the girl I remember."

Again there was silence.

"Take your time moving around the village. Raiden, you switch places with Nic."

"Gotcha."

10

It took an hour before Nic finally maneuvered himself in a position where he could clearly see all eleven hostages. His heart clenched. How could he ever mistake that chestnut hair for anybody other than Cami? Her head was hanging down as she hung from one arm from a beam of wood. Her other arm dangled from her shoulder—it had to be broken or dislocated.

He scanned the other ten people in the group. Two men were big and looked pissed as hell. They could be a real help to get the others to safety while Nic and his team took out the garbage. He said as much to the others.

"Yeah, that's what I'd thought," Raiden agreed.

"Where are all of the men in the village?" Cullen asked. "You would have thought that there would have been somebody here to defend the women and children."

The hair on the back of Nic's neck rose. "Raiden, I didn't get close enough to check out the two shacks, but there was no sign of life. I saw nothing. Can you check closer?"

"You don't think?" Raiden started.

"Yeah, I do," Nic said.

Nic swung his binoculars to the south end of the village where he could make out the shacks. Again, he couldn't see anything moving. It almost looked like they were now used for storage or something. In the dim light of dusk, Nic thought he saw a shadow and knew damn well it was Raiden Sato moving toward the shack closest to the jungle's edge.

Peering intently through his binoculars he tried to home in on Raiden, but he couldn't find him.

"Sato, what the fuck do you think you're doing?" Max growled through their comm.

Raiden didn't answer. Nic kept his eyes on the far corner of the shack, positive that Raiden would pass by there to get back to the jungle.

"Someone's coming. Get out of there." It was Cullen.

Nic saw a movement but it was just for a moment. He counted to ten in his head. At number eleven, Raiden's voice came through his receiver.

"Men and teenage boy's bodies were in the one shack I checked. They must have decimated the entire male population of the village."

Nic gripped his rifle tighter, and even though he kept his eyes open, for a millisecond he literally saw only red.

"Jesus." He heard the others' shocked responses over his receiver as he wafted a prayer up to heaven.

"Men, heads-up. Kane said he and the others will be here at zero four hundred. They're hauling ass. So, change of plans."

"We're waiting," Zed said in response.

"You got it in one," Max agreed. "So no taking out anyone, smoking or shitting in the jungle until zero three hundred. Got it?"

"Got it," they all responded.

Great, now it was a waiting game. Nic wanted to keep his binoculars trained on Cami, make sure that she stayed safe. All of those women were sitting ducks during the night.

The big man in the chair got up and stretched. "It's time for bed, tomorrow's going to be a big day. We've sent out all the e-mails today, we'll see what they have to say back. You better hope for their sake they've told me the right thing, otherwise, we're going to send them a little video of you." The students' heads nodded upwards, looking at the man. "Oh yes, you're going to be on camera for your mamas and papas. You won't like it. You won't like it at all," he laughed.

He snapped his fingers. From out of the gloom two men rushed toward him.

"Stand guard. I don't want any of them getting any idea to escape. Don't let them talk to one another."

Both men nodded. They moved closer to the tied-up students, their feet spread apart, their shoulders thrown back.

With one last look at Cami, Nic trained his binoculars on the big man to watch where he was going.

11

"I told you to shut up." The words were said in heavily accented English.

Crack. It was the sound of a hand meeting flesh. A man groaned. Who was it? Paul. Brian? It didn't sound like Travis.

"This one's not talking, she's being a good girl." This time the words were in Spanish.

"Bastardo!" It was Lisa. Then she let out a high cry. *Oh God, what now?*

"Don't, you can't untie her," a second man said in Spanish. "Whatever we do, we have to leave her tied up," the words were low, but Camilla could hear them through the gloom of the night.

"Shit, you're right. But even tied up, we can have fun," the first man said.

Camilla saw red. She knew what they were planning to do to Lisa and she couldn't let it happen. She had to stop them somehow.

"Help me!" Camilla yelled out.

"Shut up, bitch," the first man yelled out.

Nobody came over to her. Dammit, she had to get them away from Lisa.

"Help me, please somebody help me!" This time her words were in Spanish.

She heard the loud stomping of boots. Her head was pulled back with her hair, and fingers dug into her mouth, forcing it wide open.

"Uggrgh." A rag was shoved into her mouth. She tried to force it out with her tongue, but it was impossible.

"That'll shut her up. Did you do the same to the other bitch?" He was talking so fast in Spanish that Camilla was having a hard time keeping up.

"Yep," came the voice from where Lisa was hanging.

"This is even better, we each get one," the man laughed. Camilla couldn't even remember if it was the first man or the second man talking. She tried to take in air, but she was starting to choke.

"Stop this, you fuck!" It was Travis.

The man holding her laughed. "If you say another word, I slit her throat," the animal said in English. "How you like that? She dead because of you. You like that?"

Cami felt the knife at her neck while a big hand was reaching down under the waistband of her capris. She struggled wildly. She couldn't say anything, she couldn't make a sound. Listening intently, she tried to hear something from Lisa who was at the other end of the line, but there was nothing. All she could hear were the heavy pants of the man whose hands seemed to be everywhere on her. As she struggled, her injured shoulder jerked, causing the surreal moments of her impending rape to be interspersed with wild, lightning bolts of pain. Red mist swirled around her vision. She felt herself getting ready to pass out, but goddammit, she refused. There was no way she was going to stop fighting. She was *not* going to give up.

Nic had been running toward the clearing when Max's voice stopped him.

"Hale, stand down!"

How'd he even know he was moving?

"Raiden, you're in back of the church. Move to the prisoners now! The guards are getting ready to rape two of the women. I'll meet you there. We're going to stop them."

Nic pulled up his rifle and used the scope to see instead of the binoculars.

It was zero three hundred thirty. Kane and his team were still thirty minutes away. He had a perfect shot—he could take out the man touching Cami without a problem—but then they would lose all hope of a surprise. Surprise was their *only* hope. God, if only he knew that Max and Raiden would be in time to stop it, in time to...

Both women struggled. The knife that had been at Cami's neck was on the ground now and the man's hands roamed her body. Her shirt was ripped open down the front, exposing her chest. One hand kept going from squeezing one breast to the other, back and forth. Nic couldn't see the man's other hand; it was behind her back.

Nic gritted his teeth and prayed.

Cami's damaged arm flailed as she was kicking backward. Nic zoomed in so he could look closer at Cami's face. He saw the whites of her eyes, then she narrowed them. Ah, God, was she in more pain? He strained to see. No, it wasn't pain, it was rage. Pure rage.

He adjusted his focus again so he could see the whole

scene. *Where's Raiden? Where's Max?* He knew they wouldn't talk, not if they were going to be so close to the enemy. *But where in the fuck are they?* He widened his focus again to take in all eleven prisoners. He saw the other woman on the other end. She was not moving, a knife wedged under her chin. When Nic focused in on her, he saw tears running down her face. The man behind her was grinning.

Goddammit! What's taking Max and Raiden so long?

He whipped the scope back to Cami. Nic's gut clenched when he saw her slumped over. Then he realized that the man behind her was nowhere to be seen.

"Got my guy," Max Hogan whispered. "The girl is alive. She wasn't raped."

Nic was trembling when he looked back over toward the other woman. Raiden was behind the man, slowly moving around until he stood almost beside him. It was pure poetry as Raiden slid his knife into the side of the fucker's neck as he simultaneously pushed the asshole's arm forward so that the man's knife was forced away from the woman's throat, then fell to the ground.

The woman remained upright as Raiden dragged the body backward into the gloom behind the church.

"Pulling my guy into the jungle," Raiden reported. "My girl is alive," was all he said.

Nic looked at his watch; the whole op had taken ten minutes, but it had felt like a lifetime. *Twenty more minutes, then Kane and the others should be here.* Twenty more minutes, then they could rain down hellfire like no one had seen before. Twenty more minutes and he could hold Cami and never let her go.

WHAT HAD JUST HAPPENED? Am I losing my mind? Has the pain finally made me start hallucinating?

Camilla tried to lift her head, but she couldn't. It was all too much.

"Doctor Ross, are you okay?"

It was Travis.

Camilla opened her eyes and saw her bare breasts. They were black and blue. That explained the pain. Then she saw Roxanne's phone at her feet. *Oh shit.* What the hell was going to happen when El Jefe saw that? But then she closed her eyes. Who cared? What did it matter? Tears formed behind her eyelids.

"Doctor Ross?"

She didn't even care that the boy was looking at her half-naked body. Would anything matter ever again?

"Who was that man?"

At that question, she managed to lift her head and look at Travis. She opened her mouth to reply but remembered it was stuffed with a rag so she couldn't say anything. She tried to think. If Travis had seen somebody, then that meant she hadn't been hallucinating, there really was someone there. Somebody really *had* helped her.

Oh my God. People are out there. Good people.

Camilla's heart started to race. Her breathing picked up. The gag. She couldn't breathe. She couldn't catch her breath. She shook as she struggled to move her immobile arm. Why couldn't she take out her gag so she could breathe? She needed to fucking breathe!

Camilla closed her wet eyes.

Calm.

Calm.

I can do this.

Calm.

She sniffed to clear her nose, then took in a small breath. Another. Then another.

Okay, people are here. She turned her head. She could see Travis and then beside him was Roxanne, then she was pretty sure it was Jan and Paul, but she couldn't see any further down the line. She did remember that Lisa was on the end. Even in the darkness, she could see the wooden chair in front of them, the chair where that bastard El Jefe had been sitting. How much more time before he would be sitting there again, deciding their fate?

She pushed at her gag with her tongue, fighting back her revulsion at the foul taste. It started to move. She wiggled her jaw and pushed some more. She made sure to keep breathing as she continued to push out her gag.

This time, her tears were joyful when she spat the gag to the ground. *Now what?*

Okay, if they were going to be rescued, they needed to help the others help them. If that even made any sense. Camilla closed her eyes, trying to clear her head. She needed to communicate with the students. She needed to make sure they were all calm and collected if rescuers came. This was her job, and she was going to get it done, but how?

Think, Camilla!

She gazed into the darkness, trying to come up with an idea. Finally, something came to her. She'd pass down a message, but not so long that it would get lost in translation like a bad game of "telephone". Multiple short bursts.

She turned her head. "Doctor Ross says stay as quiet as possible, no matter what. Pass it down," she said to Travis.

He gave her a long look, then turned to Roxanne. She barely heard what he said to her, but she saw her head turn to Jan. Thank God, it was working! She waited three minutes.

"We're going to be rescued, and we need to be calm, quiet, and cooperate. Pass it down," she said to Travis. *Please God, let it be true.*

Travis gave her a long look of hope. He didn't ask anything, but his expression was filled with a million questions.

"Pass it down, Travis."

He nodded and turned his head.

12

KANE AND THE REST OF THE TEAM ARRIVED TEN MINUTES early.

"Status?" Kane demanded.

"We had twenty-three kidnappers," Max explained. "Of the four who were patrolling the perimeter, two have been taken out. That leaves us with twenty-one. These guys are hard-core and armed to the teeth. The prisoners are all in one place—they're staked out in front of the church. Three of them will need to be carried out by the looks of it."

"Fuck, the church is smack dab in the middle of things," Kane said. "How do you want us to position ourselves?" Kane asked.

"Zed was going to take a sniper position in the northeast corner after we did close-up wet-work, but with all of you here, he can get into the sniper position immediately. Then we'll have Ezio do the same thing from the southwest. They can act as spotters for us and then as soon as the first shot is fired they can let loose."

"The prisoners?" Kane asked. "Do they have guards on them?"

"Not anymore," Raiden bit out. "And Max, I think you're wrong, I think we have four who will need to be carried. I was hoping that some of the male students could help, but there isn't a chance in hell that their arms will be up for it after hanging on that scaffolding."

"And another thing; this isn't just a rescue, this is total annihilation," Nic interrupted. In the last twenty minutes, his eyes hadn't left Camilla. Thousands of times he'd had to force down his need to run to her. But he was a SEAL, this was a mission, he could do this.

"Nic's right. They're all dead," Max agreed. "Men, state your positions, then Leo, Kane, and Asher, position yourselves accordingly." There was agreement over Nic's receiver. "Once you're in place," Max continued, "we'll move out."

"Unless the prisoners are threatened, we save them for last. Guaranteed, they'll stir up a ruckus," Raiden said.

"Makes sense." Nic could almost hear Kane nodding over his receiver.

Nic explained over the comm where he was positioned, then he waited. He didn't hear anything, but some sixth sense told him that something was coming toward him on his left. He slowly crouched down even lower and turned his binoculars so he could scope out that area.

"Nic, it's me," Leo whispered.

Leo stood up a little taller and for a brief moment, Nic could see Leo's four-tube night vision goggles, then he was gone.

"Saw you."

"Backing up now," Leo said.

There were similar conversations between Asher and Cullen and Kane and Max.

"You all set?" Max asked.

Everybody answered in the affirmative.

"Who has the remaining two patrols in sight?" Max asked.

"I have one," Nic said. "He's walking toward me."

"I've got the other one," Cullen answered.

"Go now. Tell us when it's done, then we'll all head out with Ezio and Zed providing direction."

Nic moved slowly, making no sound as he reached the edge of the jungle. The guard wasn't even bothering to look anywhere except into the village; how stupid could he be? Didn't he understand that the threat would be coming from the jungle?

He waited for the man to go past him as Nic unsheathed his knife. As he left cover, he took six rapid steps and was behind the man in a heartbeat. He covered his mouth to ensure he didn't make a sound while he slit his throat. Nic waited until he felt the man die, then he dragged him back into the jungle. The last thing he needed was somebody noticing one of their compatriots' bodies and sounding the alarm.

"Done," Nic and Cullen said almost simultaneously.

"Zed, how many do you have?" Ezio asked.

"I've got six in my sights," Zed answered.

"I have seven," Ezio said. "I can clearly see all the way to the truck with the satellite dish. We've got one man bunked outside the truck, sleeping in the back of a Jeep. All of that is in the middle of the village."

"Shit," Zed said. "I counted that one too. That means we have eyes on twelve. So there are five unaccounted for."

"Some of them forced their way into the homes of the village women," Raiden said. His delivery was flat and unemotional. He didn't sound good.

"We'll deal with them after we have the prisoners out of

the line of fire," Max said decisively. "I didn't see any of the men go into the church, but we don't know if some of them might have been holed up in there before we arrived."

"I'm closest to the church, I'll check it out," Asher volunteered. "If it's safe, that's where we can take the hostages and that will be easy to defend while we take out the trash."

"Good plan," Max agreed.

———

WHAT PART OF 'KEEP QUIET' did Roxanne and Wendy not fucking understand? And why the hell were the others relaying their goddamn questions? If the pain in her shoulder wasn't close to making her pass out, Camilla thought the pain in her head might actually be an aneurysm caused by stupidity!

God, I shouldn't have said anything. What can I say to keep them quiet?

Lie.

I can damn well lie.

"The rescue won't start until everything is silent. We only have one chance. Pass it on." She glared at Travis as she said it. His eyes widened. He damn well better have gotten the message.

Then she heard it. The sound she'd been dreading. A bird chirping. Then, thousands of them. Oh no, how close were they to dawn? The rescue had to happen fast, otherwise, some of them were going to die, she just knew it.

Camilla tried to turn her head to the left, away from Travis, to see what was going on, but it hurt too much. Every part of her left side felt like it was on fire. This wasn't just a dislocated shoulder, it felt like her muscles were overcooked strings of spaghetti and they were barely holding her bones in place. What happened when the muscles tore and tendons snapped?

Camilla clamped her jaws shut tight over the laugh that almost escaped. *Really? You're worried about your arm when you're probably going to die?* She'd seen El Jefe and his men; there was no way people were going to be able to overtake them.

Quit being a defeatist, Ross! You're named after a goddamn Roman warrior! She turned her head again, then squinted her eyes and saw one of the guards sleeping in the back of the Jeep next to the satellite truck. She continued to scan the area, trying to find some of the other guards. She saw another sleeping with his head propped up against the wheel of the satellite truck.

Something caught her eye. She turned farther and hissed. She closed her eyes, willing away the bolt of fire that raced from her shoulder to her neck to her skull. When she could finally open her eyes again, she didn't see anything except the man in the Jeep now had his arm hanging dangling outside over the car seat. Was he dead?

"Doctor Ross?"

It wasn't Travis this time, it was Roxanne. In tiny little increments, Camilla turned her head to the right so she could look past Travis and see the girl. She didn't respond verbally, she glared at Roxanne.

"I think I saw something," Roxanne said.

"Absolute silence, or you'll ruin everything. Pass it along just to Roxanne." Camilla said the words low enough so just Travis could hear her.

If the girl had seen something, maybe she was right and

the man in the Jeep really was dead. Were their rescuers silently killing El Jefe's men just like they had killed the man who had been assaulting her? Camilla felt a surge of hope race through her.

"Doctor Ross?"

Dear God, is Roxanne even louder now?

"My phone is on the ground in front of you. What if they see it?"

There was really no help for this, was there? How in the hell could you stop it? Could she threaten to have her expelled?

Then she saw Travis whispering to Roxanne. She had no idea what he was saying, but even in this dim light, she could see Roxanne's expression begin to shift, and soon tears were tracking down her grimy face. Travis turned back to Camilla. "She'll be quiet now," he said in the quietest voice imaginable.

Camilla felt like she could breathe again.

Watching her, Travis' eyes went wide with shock. An instant later a huge hand covered her mouth.

"I'm here to help," an American man's voice whispered into her ear as Camilla felt her right arm cut loose. "Nod if you can stay standing."

Camilla nodded.

He let her go.

Damn. Without the steadying influence of the rope, Camilla lurched to the side. A solid arm reached around her waist. "I've got you."

He helped her sit down and Camilla felt the flash of pain go through her right arm now that it was lowered to her side. She longed to shake it, to dissipate the sensation of pins and needles, but she didn't want to bring any more attention to this area than they had to.

"Stay here and don't make a sound, got it?" he whispered directly into her ear.

Camilla nodded.

She watched the man as he moved to Travis. Since Travis had been watching the whole procedure, the rescuer didn't cover his mouth. Camilla didn't know what he said to Travis, but when he cut the young man loose, Travis let down his arms with a look of agony on his face, though he remained standing.

Then Travis moved over to his right and got close to Roxanne's ear as their rescuer cut her bindings. Travis grabbed both of her arms in his hands and started to massage them. Thank God for him. This just might work.

On and on down the line the man with the goggles on his helmet and the rifle strapped to his chest continued to cut down the students. When he got to Jan, who was only supported by one arm, Paul was waiting for her. He grabbed her awkwardly with his numb arms. Paul gently lowered Jan's battered body to the ground.

Finally, the rescuer got to Lisa. She was another one hanging by just one arm; God only knew how bad the cut on her arm was now. He pulled at the rope above her head and placed his knife against it to cut it.

Then all hell broke loose.

She started to kick and swing wildly. She probably would have screamed like a banshee, but she still had the gag in her mouth.

"Travis, help me up," Camilla whispered as she tried to pull her blouse closed.

He gave her a confused look.

The rescuer had cut the rope and had his arms around Lisa and was trying to lower her to the ground. Even from where she was, Camilla could see he was trying to be gentle with her, but her struggles became wilder and out of control.

Camilla held up her right hand to Travis and he grabbed it, then helped her to her feet. They walked over to Lisa and the rescuer. Camilla kept her shoulders hunched, hoping her torn blouse would hide her breasts.

Shit, the whole rescue was going to be blown if Lisa didn't get herself under control.

"Let me talk to her," Camilla whispered as she got close. The man shook his head.

"Get everybody into the church. Now. I'll take her."

Lisa was still struggling, but it didn't matter, the man's hold was implacable. Camilla turned to Travis. "Have everyone pair up who needs help, and get them into the church as fast as you can."

She would've loved to have gone down the line and coordinated the effort herself, but it was going to take all she had just to get up the four stairs to the door of the small little parish. She had to trust that Travis could take care of things.

She made it halfway to the church steps when the first shot rang out. The man carrying Lisa was already opening the church door and going in.

I can do this. Just a few more steps to the steps. Hey, I made a funny.

Camilla tried to grin at her pun, but she just didn't have it in her. Instead, she just concentrated on putting one foot in front of the other, trying to ignore the sway of her bare breasts.

Another step.

Another step.

"Ahhhh" her cry was soft. Thank God. How had she not

even seen this man? But here she was whisked up into his arms and already at the top of the church steps and he was opening the door. He set her down on one of the back pews before she had taken one proper breath, then he was gone.

13

"How's it going, Asher?" Max bit out his question over the comm.

"Half are in the church. Give me two more minutes and they'll all be there. Keep the fire away from them," he said roughly.

Nic heard the answer but processed it with only half his brain; the other half concentrated on getting himself positioned so that he could take out the two men in the truck with the tarp on it. Well, maybe there were more, but he'd seen two rifle stocks sticking out, so at least two for sure.

The problem was, if he moved from behind this Jeep there was no more cover. He opened the passenger side door and let himself in then slowly crept over the front seat until his rifle was propped over the window. His hand itched to just throw in a grenade, but he couldn't be sure that they hadn't dragged one of the village women into the truck with them, the bastards.

"I need a distraction, Ezio," Nic whispered into his mic. "Do you have eyes on me?"

"I do. You going to get whoever is in that truck, right?" Ezio asked. "Because I don't have the shot," Ezio groused.

"Yeah, I'm in position, but I need them to peek their heads out. I'm just not sure that they haven't got one of the village women in there with them, so no grenade."

"Gotcha. One distraction coming up. Maybe even three or four."

What?

Nic heard the distinctive sound of a sniper rifle popping two times, followed by cackles of chickens and squeals of pigs. Ezio must have blown out the locks on the pigpen and the chicken coop. Nic kept his sights on the back of the truck, gratified to see both men pop their heads out to see what the noise was all about.

Nic carefully aimed. Two bullets, two headshots.

"One down," Cullen said.

"I've got one," Raiden said.

"I've got two," Nic announced.

"That brings the total to eleven," Max's voice rumbled. "Asher, what's your status?"

"Everyone's in the church."

"Raiden, get your ass in there. If you need a medic back-up, let us know and we'll send in Kane," Max commanded.

"It'll take me a little more than a minute, lieutenant," Raiden said. It was obvious that he was occupied setting up a kill, otherwise, he'd be there faster.

"Okay, as soon as you can," Max agreed.

Nic backed out of the Jeep. "Ezio, what's next?" he asked.

"Two gunning at us—"

An explosion rocked Nic back on his heels. He whipped his head around to look, then cursed as he was blinded.

"Fuck, fuck, fuck." He yanked the night vision goggles

off his head then pushed his thumb and forefinger into his eyes, trying to clear them.

"A Jeep just exploded," Raiden reported. "West end of the village. Any casualties?"

Everyone reported in.

"They're trying to divert us from the villagers' homes. That's got to be it," Cullen said. "The sick fucks have been hiding out in there. I don't want any of them to get away."

Nic could see now. He didn't need the goggles since it was damn near dawn. He heard the blast of automatic fire, and then more.

"Who's on that?" Max demanded to know.

Everywhere Nic looked, there were pigs and chickens. Three doors burst open and the shooting started at a mad pace. One of the men had a woman by the neck, using her as a human shield.

The man on the right was shot down in a hail of bullets. Nic cursed; he didn't have the shot to help the woman in the middle and he knew that Ezio didn't either. He shifted his rifle to get the third man, but he'd already ducked back into the house. Someone was going to have to go in after him.

The middle man continued forward, firing short bursts as he made his way to the truck with the two men Nic had shot.

"Come to Papa," Nic murmured to himself as he crept back into the Jeep where he'd made his successful shots. The woman wasn't struggling in the least; she was worn down and defeated. Who could blame her? Nic kept his rifle trained on the man as he backed up toward the truck, continuing to shoot at nobody, trying not to trip over pigs and chickens.

Nic needed a clear shot; he couldn't have anything that

would pass through the man's body into the woman. He waited.

It was the pig that saved the day. The animal shot between the man's feet, and he stumbled. Nic made another headshot. The woman dropped to the ground and then he shot the kidnapper through the heart as well for extra insurance.

"I saw that, Hale. We're down to nine."

"Ah fuck, Max, I've got another hostage here. I've got to leave the church. Raiden, get here fast."

Another hostage? What was Asher talking about?

"You mean a villager?" Max asked.

"A kid. One of the guys is using a kid to get to the satellite truck."

"You're down to eight," Raiden reported. "Going to the church now."

CAMILLA WAS KNEELING down on the floor, the elbow of her left arm propped up on the pew, her right hand cradling that arm. Travis had found a piece of blue cloth to wrap around her shoulders that she was eternally grateful for. She no longer felt like she was being stretched out on a medieval rack. She listened as the students cried and moaned at the sounds of shots being fired, but what she really wished was that she could get over near Lisa. The woman looked catatonic. She just stared off into space; nothing was touching her.

"Lisa?" Travis called the tour guide's name. He slowly walked up to the woman who was leaning up against the side of one of the pews, her legs stretched out into the aisle.

"Lisa?" he said again. She didn't respond.

He touched her shoulder. In a shot, Lisa's arm moved with lightning speed. Her hand grabbed Travis' forearm and twisted. She looked up at him with rage. God bless Travis, he didn't make a move, didn't try to get away. "Lisa, it's me, Travis. Are you okay? We found some water, would you like a bottle?"

It was like she was looking right through him.

"Lisa," Camilla called out in her gentlest voice possible. "Can you hear me?"

Lisa cocked her head.

"Lisa, say my name. It's Camilla. Can you talk to me?"

Slowly Lisa turned her head to look at Camilla. Her eyes filled with tears. Then she looked up and saw that she was holding Travis' arm. She released it. He crouched down. "Would you like a bottle of water?"

She shrank back from him, but still managed to nod her head. "Yes, thank you." Her voice was soft and husky. This was not the confident woman from yesterday.

Still, she did manage to twist the football captain's arm...

Travis handed her the bottle, then moved to hand a bottle to the person seated in the pew next to her.

Lisa looked at Camilla. "Are you all right?" she asked as she saw how Camilla was holding her shoulder.

"I think that's my line," Camilla responded with a gentle smile.

Lisa bit her lip. "Can we focus on you?" she asked tremulously. "Or better yet, what do you think is happening out there?"

"I think our saviors are out there kicking ass and will soon be able to get us the hell out of here, that's what I think."

"Really?" Roxanne asked from the pew across the aisle.

"How many of them are there? Who are they? That man sounded like an American. How did they get here?"

Lisa winced. She slowly pushed up off the floor and walked down the aisle close to the front entrance of the church. Well wasn't that the smartest way to handle Roxanne? Too bad she had finally found a semi-comfortable way to hold her shoulder and couldn't walk away.

"Doctor Ross?"

"I'm too tired to think, Roxanne."

"But—"

"Roxanne, shove a sock in it," Travis said as he walked by to deliver another bottle of water.

"But Travis, I really want—"

"I'm serious as a damned heart attack. I'll find something to gag you with if you don't shut the hell up," the young man growled.

Roxanne's eyes welled up with tears. Camilla remembered how she had said she talked more when she was scared, but she really didn't have the capacity to care at the moment. Every time she heard another gunshot outside the church, Camilla got scared so the young woman was just going to have to learn to cope.

Suddenly Travis was crouched down in front of her. "Here, I got you another bottle of water."

"It's okay, I haven't finished mine," Camilla held up the half-full bottle. She flinched as she heard another spurt of gunfire and then pulled the cloth closer around herself.

"Okay, I'll go check on the others and see who needs some," Travis said. She couldn't turn her head to watch him go up the aisle. Instead, her gaze remained on the back of the church as she tried to drown out the sounds from outside and push away her physical pain. She started her breathing exercises: take a deep breath of pure pain-free air in through the mouth and hold it. Then blow out the pain-filled air through the mouth.

Again.

Again.

She gasped in a deep breath, spoiling her rhythm as she saw the church door open. The firefight was still going on. Who was coming inside? As soon as she saw the arm with the black t-shirt, she knew. *She knew.*

El Jefe. He swung his rifle so that it encompassed everyone in the church.

Lisa was resting against the holy water font at the front of the church. She jerked up and the man immediately spotted her. He grinned as he grabbed her by the hair.

"Hello, beautiful," he purred in Spanish. Another man came in behind them.

"El Jefe, this isn't a safe place to hide." His voice was panicked.

"We're not hiding, Raoul. We are now going to be negotiating." He raised the fist holding Lisa's hair higher and higher so that she was soon standing on her tiptoes. She whimpered in pain.

"Everyone stand up," he yelled out in English. "If you don't, I'll gut the girl, then I'll start randomly shooting you. I just need one hostage to get out of here alive, so I don't care who the hell I kill. You better play nice."

Even with this kind of threat, Camilla still didn't have the capability to turn her head and look behind her, so she just stood up and prayed that the others would as well. She saw the door open just a little, and when Maria slid in, her blood turned to ice. The woman gave a broad smile.

"Leon," she purred as she sidled up to El Jefe and put her arm around his waist. "Hiding has never looked like so much fun."

"THE CHURCH DOORS WON'T OPEN," Nic heard Raiden say over his receiver. "Asher, did you tell the kids to bar the door?"

"I didn't tell them shit. I should have."

"If I start banging on it, then that draws attention to the church and it becomes a target. How many kidnappers are we down to?"

"Five," Max answered.

"Raiden, I don't see you from my viewpoint," Zed chimed in. "But I do see a side door on the north side of the building."

"I'll move there," Raiden said.

"I'm with you. I'll be there soon," Asher chimed in. "If it's locked, I'll blow it."

Nic figured that could work, there hadn't been much activity going on in the north side of the village for the last ten minutes, so there was a good chance no kidnappers were there. Asher was their demolitions expert; it was amazing what he could accomplish with the tiniest amount of C-4.

"Why not blow the front door?" Ezio asked. He was clearly impatient. Nothing new there.

"Absolutely not. I left some of the students close to the front of the church. God knows where they are now," Asher exclaimed.

"Side door it is," Max stated, shutting down the conversation.

Goddammit, it was shitty luck that nobody had had eyes on the front of the church. How many assholes had gotten in there? What were they doing?

"I've got my eyes on three houses. One of the doors is

shut. I'm thinking some of the kidnappers could be inside," Nic said.

"That's my take too," Cullen agreed. "Which houses are you looking at, Nic?"

"I'm looking at the west."

"I've got five closed doors to the east," Cullen explained. "No real windows, they're all shuttered shut."

"Mine too."

"Each house is going to require two men as we search," Max said.

"Asher and Raiden, you continue with the church. Zed, stay in position in the tree, I want eyes on the church situation; it's fluid."

"Leo, you and Nic pair up and take the west doors," Max commanded. "Ezio, come on down and pair up with Kane. You two take the first three east doors."

"Gotcha," Ezio responded.

"Cullen, you're with me on the final two east doors. Let me know when everybody is in position, then we'll all go in at the same time. Get there fast."

Nic shut down all thoughts of the church and concentrated on his current assignment. He was sick to his stomach as to what he might find behind those closed doors after what those animals had done to the men in the village.

He ran over to the three close small homes. The first one's door was off the hinges. He had to wait for Leo—just because there wasn't a door, didn't mean that one of the damned kidnappers couldn't be in there hiding. Nic stood with his back flush up against the wall next to the door, waiting. The sun wasn't quite yet up, and he would need to be looking into small dark spaces so he engaged his night-vision goggles again.

Nic heard a subtle noise, then Leo appeared on the other

side of the door. Nic made a motion to indicate that he should go in high. Leo nodded and Nic crouched down, ready to go in low. He put up three fingers, started counting down, then...*in!*

Holy shit!

14

Every single young man in the group now had their hands zip-tied behind their backs, and zip ties around their ankles. El Jefe was having a grand old time. When he was done, he sat down beside Lisa. Once again, Lisa had that dead man's stare. She was looking at something miles away that nobody else could see as El Jefe draped his arm casually around her neck, then pressed her body in close to his.

"Maria, which one of these pretty girls would you like to have as your human shield to get the fuck out of here?" El Jefe asked in Spanish.

"I don't know. Then they get to live longer. The others will go up in smoke when we blow the church."

It finally clicked for Camilla—that's what the other man was doing as he ran around the perimeter of the church setting things down. He was setting charges.

"Yes, but it will be an easy death. Our human shields will die hard, *mi corazón*." He stroked the back of his fingers down Maria's cheek. She leaned into the caress. Camilla thought she might vomit.

"Are you choosing her?" Maria asked, pointing to Lisa.

"I think I am," he said with an oily smile. He pushed his thumbnail deep into the cut in Lisa's arm and smiled wider at her moan of pain.

Maria turned away from the pair and started to meander down the middle aisle of the church. She stopped in front of Camilla, then crouched down. "Oh, how are you, *mi pequeña*? How is your arm doing?" Maria tried to rip the cloth away from Camilla's shoulder but she held on tight, refusing to let go.

Maria slapped her across the face and Camilla lost her grip.

Maria laughed when she saw the top of Camilla's bruised breasts. "Somebody's been having fun with you, how nice." Then her avid glance turned to her bruised shoulder. She knocked her arm off the pew and Camilla cried out in agony.

"This one is defective," she said in Spanish to El Jefe. "Not her."

She got up and continued down the aisle.

Even through her misery, Camilla could hear Roxanne's pleading voice. "Please don't hurt me."

Camilla tried to stand up, tried to prove that she would be the better shield, but her legs just wouldn't seem to work.

"Shut up and come with me," Maria said harshly.

"No." Roxanne was damn near hysterical.

Camilla tried again to get to her feet. She clearly heard the slap. Roxanne let out a wail.

I hate that bitch.

There was loud scuffling and more pleading.

"Stop!" a woman's voice screeched.

"What the fuck?" Maria yelled in Spanish. Something large slammed to the stone floor.

Camilla shuddered in pain as she twisted her entire body so she could see behind her. She tried to comprehend what she was seeing. It looked like Maria was on the ground with Roxanne beside her. But Wendy and Phyllis were on top of Maria. Phyllis was sitting on Maria's chest and had one hand smashed on top of Maria's face; her other hand looked like she was trying to rip off her ear.

"You're sick!" Phyllis yelled into Maria's face.

Wendy was sitting on Maria's knees, but even that didn't stop the bitch from twisting and turning, trying to buck the two students off her.

"Stay still," Phyllis shrilled. Maria's arm shot up and hit Phyllis in the jaw, knocking her sideways.

A shot went off. Camilla jerked and saw El Jefe coming toward the melee with Lisa still clasped in one arm, his gun pointed up at the ceiling.

"I'll kill you bitches if you don't get off Maria," he hollered.

Lisa started struggling. El Jefe went down onto one knee.

Why had that happened?

That's when Camilla saw that Travis had rolled his body toward the group and he was kicking out as best he could toward the big man.

Phyllis and Wendy were no longer on Maria. She was staring down at them, a knife in her fist. Roxanne was to the side, curled up in a ball next to the pew, trying to make herself look small.

"Raoul, get over here!" El Jefe roared as he staggered to his feet. How in the hell he managed to still hold onto Lisa, Camilla would never be able to understand. When Raoul arrived, El Jefe motioned to the three women on the ground. "Pick one of these bitches up, we're getting out of here."

"This one's mine," Maria said as she kicked Phyllis in the

gut. She pulled her up by her arm and held her knife against her throat.

"I choose this one," Raoul said as he grabbed Roxanne up from the floor. Roxanne had no fight left in her; her body was limp and Raoul ended up lifting her into his arms. He walked past Maria toward El Jefe and the door. Travis' feet shot out and connected with the side of his knees. Raoul went down like a sack of potatoes right into El Jefe. Now both men and the two women were on the ground, with Maria looking at them and laughing.

"Bitch, quit laughing!" El Jefe's face was turning purple. He pushed against Lisa's chest to get to a sitting position.

Camilla heard something that sounded like an explosion, from the back of the church. Were they all going to die now? She looked at Raoul; he must have hit his head hard against the side of one of the wooden pews and he was passed out, thank the good Lord. Unfortunately, Roxanne was underneath him and Camilla couldn't tell what shape she was in.

"Raoul is a goner, we need to get out of here," Maria said as she tried to push Phyllis over Raoul's body without having her trip. "Move, bitch," she said as she shoved Phyllis forward toward El Jefe who was just getting to his feet.

The only good thing that Camilla could think was that at least they were only going to take two of them as human shields, not three of them. El Jefe was staggering to his feet.

"Where's my gun?" he asked.

Those were his last words before he was shot in the throat. Shocked eyes turned toward Lisa who was in a half-seated position, holding the gun in two hands, her eyes filled with rage. She started to change direction. Camilla knew that she was getting ready to point toward Maria, but that no good bitch kicked out hard and Lisa toppled over from the blow to the side of her head.

Maria took one frantic look around the church, then stopped and stared at Lisa, her gaze murderous. She bent over Raoul and searched the pockets on his cargo pants. She wheezed frantically, then turned his unconscious body over, shoving her hands through the pockets of his vest. She grinned when she pulled some kind of device from his pockets, then she ran to the front doors of the church. She pushed up the bar that was keeping it locked. She took one last long look at the inhabitants, then slid out the door.

The bitch had taken the detonator, Camilla was sure of it. They needed to get the hell out of there. She saw the knife on Raoul's belt; they needed it to get the ties off the boys, but there was no way she could be the one to do that. Looking around she saw that Lisa had gone into shock again, so not her. Phyllis was still on the floor with her hand on her mouth.

"Wendy!" Camilla yelled at the girl. "Grab that guy's knife and start cutting the boys loose. Start with Travis."

The girl didn't move.

A dark shadow appeared over her. Camilla let out a shriek.

"Ma'am, it's me. Asher Thorne, with the US Navy. We're getting you out of here."

"There's a bomb. We need to get out of here fast. The boys are all zip-tied."

Another man stood beside Asher, his eyes assessing. Then he was gone.

"Where's the bomb, do you know?" Asher asked.

Her arms hurt too much so she couldn't point. She tilted her chin toward the left side of the church. "Along that wall, all the way up to the Sanctuary."

"Got it." Asher left.

Maybe they wouldn't die after all.

NIC WENT in and swept the room, then stopped dead. They had not trained him for this in SEAL school. He looked at the young girl standing behind a wobbly table, using it to help hold up a gun that looked as big as she was. It was pointed directly at him. The safety wasn't on. Her little face was wet with tears, but her expression was angry and determined. Beside her was a toddler, the kid sitting on the floor in a cloth diaper, looking up at him, lost and confused.

Nic made a split-second decision. He shoved off his night goggles and laid down his rifle, then held up his hands. Somehow, he was going to have to show the girl that he was a trustworthy man.

Nic's Spanish was only so-so.

"Leo," he said softly. "I need you to have my back on this one, man."

"Jesus, son. You've gone and done it now." Nic knew that Leo had peeked around the corner.

"Help me talk her down," he said in English using his gentlest voice, not wanting to do anything to upset the girl or the baby. He felt like he was on the world's highest tightrope. Where had she gotten the gun? Oh, fuck that, who cared?

Nic stayed crouched where he was and smiled like he would at Mimi. "Hello, pretty girl. My name is Nic. What is yours?" he asked in Spanish.

She didn't move a muscle, she just continued to stare at him.

"Honey, where is your mother?"

She jerked as if he had slapped her, her brows lowered and her eyes spit fire. She stiffened her shoulders and clutched the gun tighter. Okay, so mentioning her mom was a bad thing. Dammit, he had to get her to talk.

"What can I do to help you?" Nic asked gently in his lackluster Spanish.

"Go away," the girl said.

He looked over the pistol she was holding. It was a standard Glock 357; where in the hell did she get that? He couldn't leave her alone with that.

"Leo, I need to get the gun away from her, she'll hurt herself with it," he said in English. The girl couldn't be more than ten years old. Her little arms were trembling as she tried to hold the gun up, even with the help of the table.

"Nic, just do what the hell she says. Back up and leave. It's a no-win situation."

He didn't say anything, just watched the girl as she continued to glower at him with rage, but behind that was a shit-ton of panic and fear.

The baby started to babble and reach up its arms.

"Hush," the girl said in Spanish.

The baby's babbling turned more urgent, and he or she rocked over so that it was closer to the girl, now grabbing at her leg.

"No, Theresa. Be a good baby," the girl said frantically as she looked down.

The baby turned her attention to the table leg and lunged for that. Nic made his move before there was a chance for catastrophe. In two long steps, he was at the table and plucking the gun out of the girl's hands.

"Nooooooooo," the girl wailed.

Nic heard shots.

"Got one," Max said over the comm.

"It's okay, honey," Nic crooned in Spanish to the thrashing girl. "You won't be hurt." He looked up at Leo who had the baby in his arms. "Tell her, Leo."

Leo crouched down and started talking to the girl in rapid Spanish. She responded, then he got up and flung back the sheet that separated the back of the little house from the front. Nic cursed to himself when he saw the dead woman lying on the bed.

The little girl looked at her mother and started sobbing.

"I've got one," Kane said, "and the rest of the houses are clear."

"We need a village woman over in this house, now," Nic said into his mic. "Can you help us out?"

He waited as he attempted to soothe the little girl in his arms.

"Honey, it's going to be okay," he said as he stroked her hair. She just sobbed louder. Who in the hell could blame her? Her dad and mom were both dead. In her mind, her world had ended.

Nic turned when a haggard woman rushed forward and started speaking calmly in Spanish. She rushed Leo, trying to take the baby out of his arms. Leo and the woman seemed to be arguing, then she turned to Nic and she fell to her knees in front of him.

"Give her to me," she said slowly enough in Spanish for Nic to understand.

He released the little girl into the waiting woman's arms. The little girl fell against the woman and sobbed.

15

"WE NEED TO GET THE HELL OUT OF HERE NOW," A MAN IN A military uniform said to the group. He was wearing camouflage paint all over his face.

Camilla looked up at him from where she was kneeling on the floor. She was hazy with pain, still trying to grasp the fact that they might just get out of this alive.

"Raiden, start moving them out, I haven't got this disarmed yet," the man named Asher yelled from the front of the church.

"We're going out the front doors. Raise your hand if you need help walking," the first military man said.

Camilla snorted. Hell, even raising her left hand at this point was going to be almost impossible, but she'd try.

"I've got you, Doctor Ross," Travis knelt down beside her.

"If you can help, pair up with anyone who has their hand raised. If you can't help, just haul your ass out the front door." As Camilla peeked around Travis she saw the man gently pick up Lisa.

"I can carry you too, Doctor," Travis said to her.

"I can walk. I don't want to slow you down. That way you can come back and help others," Camilla said as he helped her to her feet. The cloth fell away. Of course, it did, but she was past the point of caring. All she cared about was everybody getting out of here alive.

The first step she took with Travis' help hurt like hell. She concentrated on putting one foot in front of the other as fast as she could—anything to get out of the church so that Travis could go back inside and help others.

"Thanks, man," Travis said to Brian who was holding the church door open. He helped her down the steps.

Ahead of them, a man yelled, "Get as far as the satellite truck." She looked up and saw that it was Raiden, who was setting Lisa down so she could rest against the wheel of the truck. Paul and Jan had stopped at the bottom of the stairs but now they started to move again. She didn't see any of the other students.

"Where are the others?" she asked Travis as Raiden ran past them to go back into the church.

"Don't worry, they're coming." He positioned Camilla down next to Lisa and handed her the cloth he'd been holding. "I've got to go." Camilla watched as he ran back into the church, passing Jan and Paul. And Wendy, who was hobbling down the steps under her own steam.

She heard something off to the side, like running footsteps, and her gut clenched. She wanted to sob; here she'd thought they were safe, but now more men were coming to get them.

In the weak light of morning, she stared in horror as she counted at least five men running toward them. Wait, were there more? Six? Seven?

She tried to make herself smaller when she saw two of

them break off from the pack and run straight at her and Lisa. *Oh God, just when I thought we were safe.*

One of them skidded to a halt in front of her, the other one bent over Lisa. She reared back at the terrifying sight he made, his face covered with smears of black paint. "Ma'am, are you all right? Where are you injured? My name is Cullen Lyons with the US Navy, we're here to help you." Finally, she understood he was wearing some sort of disguise. He was a good guy. He was an American.

"Are you okay?" he asked again.

She couldn't answer. No words would come out. When she finally did open her mouth, all that came out was a sob. She bit it back and somehow composed herself, but she still couldn't manage to say a word.

He knelt down. "Ma'am?" He carefully pulled the cloth out of her clutched fingers and gently draped it around her body, his hands resting soothingly on her shoulders. That simple act of kindness broke through her wall of self-defense, and another sob escaped. And another. And another.

Even though he was still giving her comfort, he tilted his head like he was listening to something.

Camilla was somehow able to look past him and saw three more men carrying Phyllis, Roxanne, and Leslie.

Beside her, the man leaning over Lisa was talking to her softly. She seemed to be listening, but that was all.

"She's hurt," Camilla told him now that she was pulling herself together. "They cut her arm three days ago and I think it's still bleeding."

"We'll have our medic look at it." The man smiled at her.

"And you," Cullen said to Camilla. "We'll have the medic look at you too."

"What about the church?" Camilla asked. "A man set explosives."

"We got word that they've been disarmed," Cullen said soothingly.

"Huh?" That didn't make any sense. She knew Asher was inside trying to disarm them, but how would Cullen know?

He tapped a device around his neck. "Our communication system. Asher told us that he disabled the bomb."

"Where is she?" a man's voice roared from the top of the church's steps. He sounded frantic.

"Cami!" He yelled even louder.

She watched in amazement as he pounded down the steps and stood in the middle of the group of students. Camilla peered around Cullen and looked at the huge man. Power emanated off him as he looked from one student to the other.

"Cami, talk to me," his roaring voice sounded desperate. "It's me, Nic."

Nic?

Her Nic?

Camilla leaned farther, trying to see him, desperate to get a better look at him, but she couldn't tell if he was Nic Hale, not with all that paint on his face.

"Cami!"

That voice.

"Nic?" she whispered.

He whirled around. Hazel eyes lasered in on her face.

What little strength she had left deserted her, she slumped into Cullen, and he caught her. Nic came skidding to her on his knees. He thrust Cullen out of the way and pulled her into his arms.

"Cami. I've got you, baby."

She stared up at a face she didn't recognize, but clung to his voice and fell into his eyes. How was this even possible? She had to be hallucinating. Nothing this wonderful could be happening.

Camilla knew she must be close to death. She gave a deep sigh as she felt herself pressed against his strong chest, his big hands stroking down her back.

These were her last moments on earth. She was strung up with a knife slicing through her neck. She knew it, and she didn't care, because somehow she was in Nic's arms at the end.

"Cami, come out of it. Come back to me. I'm here, baby," his voice was desolate.

He cradled her close, his hold tightening. It began to hurt as he squeezed even more. She moaned.

"What is it? Where do you hurt?"

"Everywhere," she whispered to the ghost of her past. "I hurt everywhere."

"Raiden!" he shouted. The sound hurt her ears. He loosened his hold and brought up his knees so she could rest against them. He cupped her face. "Are you with me? Do you see me? Who am I?"

"You're my Nic," she whispered with a smile. "But you're not really here."

"Ah baby, you can take it to the bank that I'm here, and I'm not leaving. You're staying in my arms, by my side for the rest of your damn life."

Camilla felt herself begin to relax. Her muscles softened, her neck released and rolled to the side. It was as if all of the steel that had invaded her body since the kidnappers had boarded the bus suddenly vanished and now she was a marshmallow. She was floating on a cloud. It was a beautiful cloud because Nic Hale was with her.

"Cami, stay with me, honey." He sounded anxious. Ahhh, he didn't need to be worried when they were on the cloud.

"Raiden! Where the fuck are you, man?" Nic was yelling again.

She felt his breath on her face as he leaned in. His hazel eyes glittered; how could she have not recognized him, despite the paint on his face? Her heart should have felt his as soon as he was close.

She lifted her finger and traced the cleft in his chin. "You're here, you're really here." She breathed out the words in wonder. Hope fluttered in her soul; how was it possible that at this moment in time her dearest dream was coming true?

"I'm here, Cami," he agreed. "Just rest."

Ignoring his words, she moved her finger higher, tracing his bottom lip, glorying in the beauty that was her Nic. "I dream about you."

His eyes flared.

"Even though you didn't want me, I dream about you." She pushed her finger between his lips. She thought she heard some kind of sound in the distance but she pushed it away. She didn't want anything to disturb this moment.

Nic's eyes warmed. "After we fix you up, I want to hear about every one of your dreams. Every single detail."

He stroked her hair, just like he used to. Camilla tried to lift her other arm so she could encircle his neck. As soon as she did, fire flared and she moaned with pain.

Nic pulled her finger out of his mouth. "Cami, you need to stop. You're injured, baby. Let me take care of you. Don't move."

A wave of sound crashed down upon her. She blinked and saw she was surrounded by men in uniform and the other students. Her breath shuddered as she took in where she was, then she looked back up at Nic and clutched at his shirt.

"It's okay Cami, I'm here. I've got you."

"Don't leave me," she begged desperately. "Don't leave me again, please."

"I won't. I promise."

He turned his head and shouted. "Raiden, get your ass over here."

A man knelt down beside them. "Raiden's with the tour guide. You're stuck with me."

"Kane, she's in bad shape. You've got to help her."

Camilla kept staring at Nic, praying she could stay in his arms.

"Miss, you're going to be just fine. Nic won't let anything bad happen to you again."

16

He wanted to be holding her in his arms, but right now other things needed to be done.

"The choppers should be here by nightfall," Max said as he looked down at Kane's tablet. "Thank God we don't have any life-threatening injuries. Just the same, they'll be ready to help with the injured."

"I don't like the look of Lisa's arm," Raiden said. "She definitely has a fever and infection."

"I hear you," Max said soothingly. "Also, Camilla Ross needs surgery. Her shoulder is barely holding together. But still, they'll both be fine for the twenty-four hours it'll take to get them to a hospital in the States."

Nic knew it was true. When they'd finally tried to move Cami, it had become clear just how much pain she'd been in. Kane had had to administer a shit-ton of painkillers to help her out, now she was resting in the back of the satellite truck along with Lisa, Jan, and Phyllis. It looked like it might rain, so they wanted to keep them covered.

"Raiden, how are the others looking?"

"You're right Max, no other life-threatening injuries.

They are all resting as comfortably as possible. I'm going to go join Kane and see to the villagers." He turned and left at a run.

That just left Max and Nic.

"How are you doing?" Max asked.

"Worried as hell about Cami, but also like it's the best day of my life," he grinned at his lieutenant.

"I'm going to have you airlifted with the students. The rest of us are going to stick around and help the villagers. We'll wait for the federales, then call in choppers."

His relief was palpable. "Thanks, Max."

"No problem."

LOGICALLY, Nic knew Cami was going to be all right, but every minute she was in surgery was hell. They'd flown into Miami last night, and the surgery had started first thing this morning. He was surprised that Cami's parents still hadn't arrived—surprised but relieved.

A doctor came into the waiting room and he stood up. She looked around and saw a two groups of tired families, him and Paul Davis. "Who is here for Lisa Garcia?" she asked.

Nic stood up.

She looked at him warily. He could understand why. He'd borrowed a clean t-shirt from one of the guys on the helicopter, then he'd tried to clean up as best as he could in the hospital bathroom, but there was only so much you could do with hand soap and paper towels.

"Yes, I'm here for Lisa," Nic answered automatically. "How is she?"

"She's doing as well as can be expected. We have her on

a high dose of intravenous antibiotics. Her fever is still pretty high. We're going to keep her with us until we think it's safe for her to travel. Her arm was badly infected."

"Is there any word on Camilla Ross or Jan Hines?" he asked as he looked over at Paul.

"Were you one of the students on the bus?" she asked as she gave him another once over.

"No, ma'am."

He could see the lightbulb go off over her head. "You were part of the rescue team, weren't you?"

He nodded.

"I can't tell you about anybody else. Lisa is my only patient." She looked around the waiting room again. "Did y'all contact their relatives?"

"The authorities are getting in touch with them, yes, ma'am."

"I hope they get here soon. Lisa could use some familiar faces around her. When they arrive, have them check in at the nurses' station."

Nic nodded and the doctor left.

Nic thought about what he had seen the other night when Lisa had been strung up and the guard had been mauling her. Damn straight she needed her family. He needed to make some calls to find out what was keeping them.

So many parents had descended like locusts on the hospital starting last night. The last students who still didn't have family here were Jan Hines and Cami.

"I'm going to go ask about Jan again," Paul said as he stood up and faced Nic.

"You're just going to piss off the nurses," Nic told the kid. "Why don't you go to the hotel where your dad's staying?"

"He was wrecked. He needs to sleep. He'd been up

almost the entire time I was missing. I need to be here and see how Jan is doing," the kid said emphatically. Nic couldn't blame him. He looked down at his watch again. Cami had been in surgery for three hours now, what in the hell was taking so long?

"Nic Hale?" A tall blond man walked into the waiting room. Nic looked over at him. He didn't know him, but he knew him. He'd bet his next paycheck that the man was Special Operations.

Nic nodded. "That's me," he said cautiously.

The man smiled easily. "The name's Jack Preston. I flew over from my ranch in Texas to keep you company. Your lieutenant called my lieutenant." He spoke with a Texas drawl and there was compassion in his voice.

Paul gave them both the side-eye. "I'm going to the nurses' station," he said before he left the room.

Nic nodded toward the chairs in the corner and Jack followed him. They sat down.

"So Max called who and why?" Nic asked.

"I'm pretty sure I'm here to babysit you." Jack grinned. "Don't take it bad, I've had members of my team sit on me like they planned to hatch an egg, so I know what this is like."

Nic shook his head. "Look, I'm running on too little sleep, the chicken references are confusing me. Can you be more specific?"

"Your woman is hurt and in surgery, right?" Jack asked kindly.

Nic nodded.

"Your lieutenant, Max Hogan, called my lieutenant, Mason Gault, and asked if he had anybody close by who could come sit with you, that's all."

Nic pressed his thumb and forefinger into the bridge of

his nose, trying to comprehend everything. He looked up and Jack was just sitting there, looking comfortable in the visitors' chair with an easygoing expression on his face, waiting for Nic to make up his mind about him. Nic felt some of the tension drain out of his body.

"No disrespect, but Texas isn't exactly close by."

"I have a plane, it wasn't a problem. Never mind about me. Let's focus on you and your lady."

"You ever been in a situation like this before?" he asked Jack.

"I've been in a Texas hospital before, waiting to see if my woman would live or die." Jack looked grim for a moment.

"And?"

"She's my wife now. We've got two beautiful little girls."

"That's good. That's real good." Nic smiled. "This isn't life or death; her shoulder is all sorts of fucked-up. Our medic said they were going to have to spend a lot of time repairing torn muscles and ligaments. He told me to expect a long surgery." Nic shook his head, still trying to understand. "If you're from Texas, why are you here in Florida?"

"Disney World. We're here on a family vacation. So, when did the surgery start?" Jack asked.

"A little over three hours ago."

"Have you eaten?"

Nic shook his head.

"Then I'll go get you something to eat, and not something from the hospital cafeteria, either."

Paul walked back into the waiting room, muttering to himself.

"Paul," Nic said, getting the young man's attention. "This is Jack. He's offered to get us some food. You in?"

Paul looked up, his face brightening. "Absolutely I'm in."

Jack stood up. "Anything else that you two need?" Jack asked.

"Yeah," Nic said. "My computer guru is still in Mexico finishing some things up. From what I'm hearing the authorities are having a hard time locating any family members for Lisa Garcia; she's the tour guide on the bus. She's here in the hospital and will be for a couple of days. Do you have someone who could do a search?"

Jack grinned. "Consider it done," he said as he took his phone out of his back pocket. "I'll be back with food and hopefully some information in less than an hour."

Hell, if it was going to be that easy, Nic thought, *maybe I should have had him track down Cami's parents. What in the hell is taking them so long to get here?*

"CAMI, CAN YOU HEAR ME?"

Only Nic had ever called her Cami and she loved it. It made her feel safe. Cherished.

"Baby, can you wake up?"

She didn't want to wake up, this was a good dream. She'd been having really bad dreams, but this was a good one. There was no pain, and instead of angry voices, she was hearing Nic's kind voice. No how, no sir, she didn't want to wake up.

A butterfly landed on her cheek. Its wings brushed softly against her skin, back and forth. Camilla was afraid to disturb the butterfly but she couldn't stop herself from leaning into the touch. She sighed with pleasure as the caress deepened.

"That's it, feel me. Come back to me. I love you so damn much, and I want to see those gorgeous baby blues."

Camilla smiled and thought about lifting her eyelids. It would be such a pleasure if she could actually see Nic again. It would be one of her dearest fantasies come to life.

"Please, Cami," he coaxed.

She opened her eyes and saw Nic's smile. She smiled back and her eyes started to overflow with tears. He was so beautiful.

"Hi, Nic." That didn't sound like her voice.

She coughed once, and then again. Soon she was coughing repeatedly.

"Careful, honey." He brought a cup with a straw to her lips and she took a sip.

"Better?" Nic asked.

She took another sip.

"Now I'm better." Her voice was rough and husky. She tried to stretch, then she winced. Looking down she saw that her arms were immobilized. One was in a cast, the other had bandages on it. She felt bandages around her chest. Her face hurt.

The jungle.

El Jefe.

Her eyes went wide. "You saved me, Nic. You're a rescuer."

He tenderly brushed the hair back from her face. "Something like that," he agreed. "Are you remembering what happened?"

"We were kidnapped when we were on the bus." She bit her lip, then let out a little cry at the sting. "Liz died. So did Haley." Her tears started in earnest.

"It's going to be all right," he whispered.

"Michael and Larry died too." Her tears were falling even faster.

"I so wish I could hold you, but if I did, I'd hurt you." He cupped her cheeks and brushed kisses along her temple, her cheek, her jaw.

When her weeping seemed to have run its course, Nic found some tissues, wiped up her tears, and then pressed the tissue against her nose.

"Blow, honey."

She did and she could breathe again. She relaxed her head back against the pillows and stared up at Nic. "I don't understand, Nic. How is it possible that you were there to get us?"

Nic sat down in the chair next to her bed and moved it even closer. He kept one hand resting against her jaw.

"I'm a Navy SEAL, baby. Our mission was to go into the jungle and bring all of you out alive."

"Oh yeah, you wanted to be a Navy SEAL like your dad was. So you did it."

"Yeah, I did it," he nodded.

She closed her eyes, so many memories came flooding back to her at the mention of the Navy. She remembered flying into Chicago and going to the Navy Training Center, only to be sent away. She remembered calling and calling and sending letter after letter, only to have them come back return to sender.

He'd cut her out of his life like some kind of cancer.

"Hey, don't go there," Nic pleaded.

"Don't go where?" Camilla asked bitterly. "Don't remember your utter and total rejection of me? You threw me away. I was eighteen and I loved you desperately. I wanted to make a life with you. I wanted to marry you. I would have followed you anywhere, done anything to stay with you, but you abandoned me."

"Cami, be fair, I always said we weren't going to get married until you finished college."

It was a hit. It was a hit and she wouldn't acknowledge it. She'd planned for every contingency. She'd arranged everything. She'd had every school lined up, why couldn't he have just gone along with it? She was back in her eighteen year old body, wrapped up in her young tender emotions and it killed.

"You abandoned me." Her voice sounded so young.

"I was always going to come back to you. Always."

She blinked, her eyes cleared and she saw the man in front of her. "But you didn't come back to me."

She saw the panic on his face and it made no sense.

"Cami, I tried to explain in my letters. Why didn't you at least open them?"

She laughed, and regretted it, as pain shot through her chest. "There were no letters Nic. And if there were, shouldn't I have just sent them back return to sender, wasn't that how it was done?" She heard the pain in her voice, and it wasn't from her injuries.

She was watching him closely, and the metamorphosis was profound, he went from panicked to resolute.

"There were letters, there were ten of them. You'd just finished your junior year. I know because that was when I got my trident. And you did send them all back to me, return to sender. I explained everything to you. Why I made the choice I did, and how I hoped we could make a future together. I laid my heart bare."

She stared at him confused. She knew Nic, he'd never been a liar. Not ever.

His eyes narrowed as he looked at her. They needed to talk this out, it was important. She rolled to her side so she could sit up.

"Ahhhh," the pain hit like lightening she pressed down on her right side.

Nic crouched down beside her in an instant, helping her roll to her back.

"Jesus Cami, what were you thinking?"

She couldn't think, she could only feel. And whimper.

"Honey, I'll be right back with a nurse." Suddenly the room was empty. Her eyes were wet as she tried to think through everything he had been saying through the mist of pain. Ten letters?

The door opened, she didn't recognize the nurse who came in before Nic but it didn't matter, Camilla knew she would do something for her pain. The entire time she fiddled with her IV tube Nic watched on in solemn silence.

"Thank you," Camilla said as the nurse started to leave.

"It's no problem. Don't forget, you have a call button by your bed, you use that any time you need to."

Camilla nodded.

Then she and Nic were alone. She knew she didn't have much time before the pain meds started working.

"I didn't get any letters Nic."

"Don't worry about it. We're just going to move forward, okay?"

The first wave of dizziness hit. The pain began to dissipate.

"I can't think right now. Seriously, I can't handle any of this. Can we do this some other time?"

He gave her a considering look.

"Please Nic," she said quietly. "I need you to leave."

"Okay honey, I'll leave now, but I *will* be back. I love you Cami."

She watched him walk out the door.

17

SHE HEARD THE CLICK OF THE DOOR CLOSE BEHIND HIM. SHE didn't have any tears left. She stared at the white hospital wall. Memories assailed her. Not of the jungle. Of course not. It was the one precious memory that always came to her. It was Nic. Always Nic.

"CAMI, your heart is beating a million times a minute," he said as he pressed a warm kiss against the pulse in her neck. "We don't have to do this."

Her laugh didn't sound like her, it was rich and husky. "You don't know how many times I've imagined us here at this point, naked, in one another's arms. Of course, my heart is beating fast, I've never been so excited. This is my every dream come true."

Camilla stroked her hands along the back of his broad shoulders, then drifted them down his back until they sank into the firm flesh of his ass. Perfection.

Nic grinned down at her, his hazel eyes flashing. "So you're not going to have any maidenly vapors?"

Another husky laugh. "Where did you ever hear that?" she asked as she squeezed his ass again.

"I don't want to talk about some show mom was watching on cable," Nic said. Slowly, he lifted his body up from hers so that she could see him from the top of his chest to his groin. Maybe she was going to have maidenly vapors.

Her hands were now laced around the back of his neck, she looked into his eyes, but they were focused elsewhere.

"God Cami, you're so fucking beautiful."

She could feel the blush start from her toes and go all the way up to her face. Every part of her body was heating up.

"I want to touch you," she said as she pushed at his chest. Nic grinned down at her.

"You are touching me."

"Down there," she whispered. "Now shove over so I can." She pushed harder and he rolled over onto his back.

"So little Miss Pushy Pants, you have no problem manhandling the goods, but you can't say the word cock?"

She watched avidly as Nic circled his flesh with his fist and stroked it up and down. He shuddered and so did she. She moved closer so she could see better, her fingers twitched, she so badly wanted to touch him.

"Cami, talk to me. Is this too much for you?"

"No," she exclaimed. "Well maybe," she said slowly as she licked her lips. "Nic, I know it's going to hurt the first time, but I feel all achy. It's been hurting a lot not doing it."

His head shot up to look at her face.

"Achy?"

"I think about this a lot." She grabbed his wrist, wresting his hand away from his erection. She knelt up on the bed, loving how his eyes followed her every move. He changed positions so that he was kneeling in front of her. Waiting. For long moments they stared at one another.

"What do you want? Name it and it's yours," he asked.

She drew his hand down so that he could touch the folds of her sex. Her entire body jerked; it was like she'd touched a live electrical wire. Nic's other hand cupped her cheek.

"Stay with me Cami," he whispered. His fingers stroked her tender flesh, up and down he followed the seam of her sex. Cami held her breath, waiting for a deeper touch and he didn't disappoint her. When one of his big fingers probed deep she gasped and grabbed his shoulders.

"You're so soft and wet. You feel so good, Cami."

"I do?"

He looked back up so she could see his eyes. They were almost emerald green with desire.

"Baby, I need you to lie down, can you do that for me?"

Part of her wanted to argue. They were in this together, so she would only lie down if he did, but there was something in his face that made her comply. His arm wrapped around her back to help lower her to the mattress. His finger never stopped stroking inside her body.

"We're going to take this slow," he said with a tight smile.

"I don't want to go slow, I want you now." She reached out to touch his erection.

"No Cami, don't touch me. If you do I'll explode like a rocket. Keep your hands on my shoulders. Just let me pleasure you this first time, okay?"

She could see his need and anxiety, and it got through to her like nothing else could have. She relaxed back into the mattress, her hands by her head, and let the sensations wash over her. Nic bent his head to her breast. He licked all around her nipple then blew. She arched off the bed as he pressed two fingers inside her body.

"What?"

He sucked her hardened tip into his mouth and she moaned.

Fire ripped through her blood, sparks sizzled down every vein as she tried to make sense of what she was feeling. Dimly she realized she'd spread her legs wide in a wanton need for more.

She was so close to the pinnacle, an orgasm like no other, when Nic pulled his fingers out of her heated channel and knelt up higher.

"No!" She lifted her weak arms and tried to pull him back to her.

"I'm here Cami, I'm not leaving."

She heard the crinkle of a foil wrapper and realized he was protecting her. When wasn't he protecting her? She watched as he sheathed his erection and moved over her, one arm cuddling her head, his eyes looking into hers.

"I love you so much. You're my world." He blessed her with a tender kiss that soon turned hot and wild. Camilla lifted her knees, trying to tempt him into her body. He swept his hand down until he was touching the curls at the apex of her thighs, but that wasn't what she wanted.

"No, I want your...your..."

"Say it, honey," he grinned down at her. "The word is cock."

She balled up her fist and hit him on his shoulder. Hard. "Fine, you smartass, I want your cock." She whispered the last word, she couldn't help it.

His laughter sighed out of him. His hand moved past her curls and then she felt his thumb touching her clitoris.

"Ahhhhh." White shone behind the backs of her eyelids. It wasn't quite the right touch that she needed at first, but Nic being Nic, learned quick. Soon he was circling her swollen bud and she was panting and struggling to keep herself under control.

"Stop it! I need you inside me. We get to make love, you promised." She felt tears dripping down her temples. She stared up at him, seeing the indecision on his face. "Nic, it's going to be

all right. I promise. How could anything we do together ever really hurt me? Our bodies were meant to be together."

He continued to circle her clit as he positioned his cock at her swollen entrance. Camilla willed herself to relax. When he started to enter her it was everything she could have hoped for—he was stretching her, filling her, making her feel complete. Then he pressed even farther, and the sensation changed. Her body was trying to stop him, trying to keep him out. She looked up at Nic's face that was tight with concentration.

He started to pull out.

"Cami—"

Using her knees she shoved up with all the strength that she had.

"Uggh," she muffled the sound as quickly as she could by pressing her mouth against his neck.

Dammit, she felt even more tears leaking from her eyes. She was a damned faucet, and it was going to scare the hell out of Nic.

"Cami. Look at me."

She took three deep breaths and the pain drifted away. It was like it had never happened. Instead, she was connected in the most primal way possible to the man she loved. She pulled back so she could look into his eyes and smiled.

He searched her face. She knew what he saw—nothing but love.

A slow smile spread across Nic's face. She felt him pulse deep inside her and her eyes widened.

"Are you ready?" he asked.

"I'm ready for anything." She grinned. She gasped as he slowly retreated, his cock caressing every part of her, then he pushed back inside just as slowly, watching her intently. Had anything ever felt so good?

"That's my line," he smiled.

She must have said that out loud.

He continued to caress her channel with delicious strokes of his cock. She gulped in a huge breath when he pressed even deeper, then pulled back out, scraping against a magical place.

"Again," she begged.

His strokes got faster and stronger, and her legs wrapped around his waist. He moved the hand that had been beside her head and slid it down her body until he was once again touching her clit.

It was too much pleasure, but she greedily grasped every bit of it. She looked up into his handsome face, memorizing him, memorizing this perfect moment in time.

"I want everything," she begged. "I want you to give me all of you."

She loved his look of surprise.

"Let go, Nic. I want us to fly together."

It was like she had unleashed a thunderstorm. His kiss was ferocious. His tongue delved deep, exactly matching the rhythm of his cock, his chest glided against her breasts, making her nipples feel like they were going to burst.

Higher and higher he pushed her. So high she could see the clouds, the sky, the stars.

She burst through to the edge of the galaxy, lost in wide emerald green eyes that were dazed with pleasure.

"You're my everything, Cami," he whispered as his thumb traced her bottom lip. "My everything."

18

"WHAT TOOK YOU SO LONG TO GET HERE, MRS. ROSS?"

It was Nic's voice, and he sounded pissed. Wait, she'd told him to leave, hadn't she?

"I had to give a speech, if you must know. I've been in constant contact with Camilla's doctors as soon as she was admitted. If I thought her situation was critical, of course, I would have canceled and come immediately."

"Where's Mr. Ross?"

Oh, he sounded so pissed. She needed to open her eyes. This was not good.

"Clifford is on a dig. I contacted him, but it will be a couple of more days before he can get here."

"Jesus Christ, you people are fucking amazing."

"Nic," Camilla called out as she opened her eyes. "What are you doing here?"

"Camilla, you're awake." Her mother walked over to her side before Nic had a chance to answer. "How are you feeling? The doctor said you might need to have another surgery, he's not sure, it depends. The damage was extensive."

Camilla looked into eyes that were a mirror of her own. "Hello, Mother. What country is Dad in?"

"Mongolia. He should be here the day after tomorrow, that is if you're still in the hospital. I think it would be best if you came home for a little while. I don't think you're in any condition to take care of yourself. I can hire in a nurse."

So much for tender loving care. No questions about the kidnapping. Nada, zip, nothing. You would have thought a scientist would have had more curiosity.

"Mother, I can just as easily arrange for a nurse in my own apartment."

"Nonsense, everyone would expect you to be staying with your father and me."

Ah-ha, now everything makes sense; she doesn't want to lose face with her university friends.

"She can stay with me," Nic said as he stepped up beside her mother. "I have plenty of leave I can take so it wouldn't be a problem at all."

Before Camilla could respond to his offer, her mother turned on him. It didn't seem to bother her that she was a foot shorter and probably a hundred pounds lighter than him, she was going to have her say. "I don't know how you even found out about Camilla's ordeal, or how you came to be here, but you are surely not involved. You should never have been involved with my daughter from the beginning. The best thing that ever happened was the day you disappeared and were never heard from again."

"Mother." Camilla was aghast. She'd known that her dad and mom disapproved of Nic years ago, but never to this extent. "Do you know what Nic did? He and his teammates risked their lives to save me and the other students. He's a hero."

Enid Ross looked like she had sucked on a lemon. "He's

just a glorified thug that our government has on the payroll to do their dirty work."

She knew that her mother was an elitist but she'd never heard her like this before. It was profoundly upsetting. How could she have been raised by this woman?

"Mother, Nic serves our country. I am proud of what he does. He is an honorable man, and he helped to save eleven lives two days ago."

"Camilla, I'm not going to argue semantics with you. I came here to talk about your recovery. Your shoulder is going to require a great deal of time to heal, and then there will be months of rehabilitation. I have no idea when you can go back to your job at the university. We need to develop a plan for your future."

"Jesus lady, you can't possibly be worried about Cami's career right now. She was just kidnapped. You can't possibly understand what she's gone through. She needs a hell of a long time to just recover from that."

"Nonsense. My daughter is strong. She can rise past that. It's her physical well-being that I'm concerned about."

Camilla watched Nic's incredulous expression. She wanted to laugh. She remembered spending time at his parents' house—the times when his parents had been there—and she had loved them. They had been so warm and welcoming. It was a whole different dynamic at the Hale household. Camilla had almost been embarrassed to introduce Nic to her parents, and her mother was proving why again. But the woman *was* her mother, and Camilla wouldn't have expected anything different.

"Mrs. Ross—"

"It's *Doctor* Ross," she interrupted.

"If you're a damned doctor, then you should really

understand that Cami needs love and support right now, not to be railroaded by some unemotional robot."

"I'm a doctor of physics, not a medical doctor."

Camilla swallowed a laugh. Really, that's what her mother wanted to defend herself about?

"If Camilla would allow it, I want her to come home with me, so I can take care of her."

"Wait a moment, did you just ask me, Nic? Was that an actual question, not an edict?"

He rubbed the back of his neck and grimaced. "Actually, it was a plea. Please Cami, come to my place."

"That's utter nonsense. Camilla, you haven't heard from this boy since he left you years ago, why in the world would you even consider allowing him to have anything to do with you now?"

Boy?

"Mother, can we sort this out some other time. It's too much for me to take in right now."

"Fine. I'm going to check in with your doctor, maybe even your surgeon, and then I'm going to my hotel. I will come and visit you as soon as visiting hours begin tomorrow morning. You've had enough fuss for one day."

"I'll see you tomorrow morning then." Camilla nodded. That was when it occurred to her that her mother hadn't even touched her during the entire visit. She watched as her mother turned toward the door.

"Nic, come along," Enid said, looking back at the man who was standing next to her bed.

"I'm not leaving unless Cami asks me to."

"Her name is Camilla."

Camilla looked up at Nic's face. Her dream was uppermost in her mind—she just couldn't let him go.

"It's okay, Mother, he can stay."

"As you wish," she clipped out. Then she let herself out of the room.

NIC LOOKED DOWN AT CAMILLA. There were bruises on her face. Between the massive bandages that started up at her neck and went down to her right elbow to the smaller bandages on her left arm she almost looked like a mummy.

"Thank you for letting me stay," he said. She didn't respond. "Why *are* you letting me stay?" he finally asked.

"Lots of reasons. Who you were back then, the man you are today. The man who put his life on the line for people he didn't know. Take your pick."

Her blue eyes studied him. He remembered that, how she used to watch him. It had been like she was trying to get under his skin and understand exactly what made him tick. It had amused him back in high school because even he hadn't known what made him tick back then.

She didn't say anything else, and finally, he blurted out what had been eating at him.

"You're not married. Your name is still Ross. I don't see a ring."

She frowned. "No. Are you?"

"Nope, never been. And you? Ever been married that is?"

She was still frowning up at him. He wanted an answer. Not just to this, but to everything. He wanted to know about every single day of her life since he had last seen her. But first, he wanted to know about Harris Prescott, the man she'd been engaged to.

"No, I've never been married, not even close."

What the hell?

"That's not true, Cami. You were engaged."

Wide blue eyes met his. "I was never engaged," she denied.

"Does the name Harris Prescott ring a bell?" He kept his voice soft and even. There wasn't a chance in hell that he was going to be anything but gentle with this woman who had been mauled two nights ago. But at the same time, he wasn't going to let this slide, either.

Camilla rolled her eyes. "Oh him. According to Mother and Dad, I was engaged all right. He's an archeologist who worked with Dad. He asked me to marry him. I put him off, but as far as my parents were concerned it was a done deal. They even put an announcement in the paper. But no, I've never been engaged."

What in the ever-loving hell?

Nic reached behind him and his fingers touched the chair. He tugged at it and sank down.

"Are you okay?" she asked him. She shifted in the bed, trying to turn so she could see him better, and winced.

"Stop, don't hurt yourself, baby."

Nic gave her a strained smile. Now was not the time to go into the shit of their past. Right now she needed to focus on getting better, and by God, he was going to be the one to take care of her.

"How did you know about Harris?" she asked him.

It was his turn to wince. "I saw that engagement announcement," he admitted. He just wasn't going to tell her how he got his hands on it. "But let's not worry about that right now, we've got bigger things on our plate. I've visited my teammates when they've been in the hospital, and I've got to say, you are showing all the classic signs of being in pain, am I right?" He offered up his most charming grin.

"But I want to know—"

"Later, Cami, I promise. But right now I want to make sure you're taken care of. Let me call a nurse so she can give you something for the pain, okay?"

Again with that blue-eyed stare that he swore could read his heart, but she finally nodded. "Yes, call the nurse."

He got up from the chair, then bent over and touched his lips to her forehead. "I'll be right back."

By the time he watched Camilla settle into a pain-free sleep, Nic realized he was exhausted. He damn near stumbled to the waiting room, remembering he had left his backpack with Jack Preston.

Jack stood up and smiled.

"Here's your room key," Jack Preston said as he handed Nic a key card.

"Huh?" Nic looked down at the piece of plastic in his hand like he had never seen anything like it before.

Jack put his hand on Nic's shoulder and started to push him out of the waiting room toward the elevator. "It's night-night time for you. I've got you checked in at the hotel two blocks away. You, young man, need some shut-eye. A shower and a change of clothes wouldn't be a bad thing either, because you kind of stink."

Nic blinked at the other SEAL, trying to make sense of what he was saying. Jack kept on talking as he led him through the hospital lobby and out into the parking lot to a big truck. "Hop on in," he motioned.

Jack put the truck into gear and started to slowly make their way through the parking lot. "So was that your future mother-in-law that I saw chewing up some poor doctor?"

Nic shook his head, trying to clear it. Damn, he was tired.

Jack laughed. "Never mind, just flipping you shit. It's really not fair in your condition. Let's get you to the hotel and in the morning I'll get you the information you wanted about Lisa Garcia."

"Oh right," Nic remembered. He felt bad that he hadn't checked up on her status. He was totally losing it.

"I checked up on her," Jack said as if he were reading Nic's mind. "She's still being pumped up on antibiotics while the docs watch her status. They don't see any reason she won't make a full recovery."

"That's good," Nic said as he yawned. He refused to close his eyes.

Jack pulled up to the front of the hotel and waved off the valet. "Okay, sleeping beauty, this is your stop. Your pack is in the backseat. I put in some clean clothes for you to wear. The room is paid for through the end of this week."

Nic was getting out of the front seat when Jack's last words sank in. Those woke him up.

"Man, I can cover the room."

Jack grinned. "Trust me, it's not a problem. Look up the Preston Ranch in Texas some time, and you'll see I can afford it. I need to get back to the ranch, then I'm back to Coronado."

Nic leaned in and offered his hand. Jack shook it. "Take care of yourself, and take care of your woman."

"I intend to."

RAIDEN SLIPPED INTO THE SEAT BESIDE HIM. ON SOME PRIMAL level, Nic had been expecting this. Still, he had to ask.

"I thought the team was going straight back to Little Creek."

"I wanted to check up on some things," Raiden said. His trademark smile was nowhere to be seen.

"You want the four-one-one on Lisa?"

"Kane's already given me everything there is to know about her status here at the hospital."

"I've got more info," Nic said.

Raiden raised his eyebrow. "Tell me."

"Nobody ever came here to claim her. It was pissing me off, so I had Midnight Delta's version of Kane do a deep dive. Her parents are dead, she was raised by her grandmother, who passed three years ago. No siblings. No boyfriends or girlfriends. She's your quintessential loner."

"How about people from her old work?"

"The wilderness trekkers?" Nic asked. "No, that was a dead-end too. According to the woman who ran the company, Lisa did have a lot of friends, but nobody really close. Then she just up and quit two years ago. Nobody knew where she went."

"Hmmm."

"You know visiting hours aren't for another forty-five minutes, right?" Nic asked.

"Yeah," Raiden gave him a sideways look. "But I was pretty sure you'd be here."

"You could have called," Nic mentioned.

"Sure could have. Wanna go grab some coffee?" Raiden was almost smiling. "Now that you've filled me in on Lisa you can fill me in on your Cami."

"First I want to know how it went with the women and kids at the village," Nic said as they headed out to the elevators.

Raiden blew out a breath and rubbed at his jaw. "It was hard, Nic. Really fucking hard. We only had to wait twenty-four hours for the Mexican federales and aid workers to fly in, but in the meantime, we did what we could. One of the women died on my watch."

Nic didn't respond—after all, what could he say? He just led Raiden toward the cafeteria. "Why don't you go get us a table, I'll grab the coffees."

Raiden nodded.

Nic went through the early morning line, mingling with mostly hospital staff. He thought about what Raiden said. The little girl who'd held a gun on him and her baby sister had broken his heart. What was she going to do without a mother and father? The village might have seemed poor and in the middle of nowhere, but it had been a little community of people who prayed, loved, and supported one another and it had been ripped apart.

"Sir?"

Nic looked up at the cashier and realized she was waiting for him to pay.

"Sorry," he pulled money out of his wallet and handed it to her. She gave him a tentative smile. He must not have been giving off a very good vibe. *I better pull it together before I see Cami.*

Nic spotted Raiden sitting in the corner with his back against the wall. He deposited the black coffee in front of him, along with packets of sugar and cream. He pushed his chair sideways so he had a good view of the room but could still talk to Raiden.

"Do you know what happened to the little girl who had the gun on me?" he asked.

Raiden's lip ticked upward. "Yeah, Leo told me about that. He pointed her out to me. They brought in some damn good people to help. I saw one of the nurses talking to her. I can tell you she wasn't being ignored, you know?"

"What do you think is going to happen to her and the others? A lot of those kids have to be orphans now."

Raiden looked at him from under his brows. "Kid, you can't solve the world's problems."

If only he had a dime for the number of times he'd heard that, he'd be rich.

"Seriously Nic, concentrate on what you can take care of. Concentrate on Cami."

"I want to take her home with me. I want to take leave and take care of her."

Nic spun his coffee mug around, looking at the brown liquid, trying to figure out how he was going to get her to agree to his idea.

"And her parents?" Raiden asked.

"They're ice cold. I don't know how someone as warm and loving as Cami came from two people like them, it makes no sense. But I'm going to have a battle on my hands with her mother."

"Is she here?"

"She will be. She said she'd be here when visiting hours started this morning. I just can't wait," he said sarcastically.

"What does Cami want?" Raiden asked as he took a sip of his doctored coffee.

"She already said she doesn't want to stay with her parents. She was making noise about staying in her apartment and hiring a nurse. Over my dead fucking body."

"Glad to see you have some perspective on the whole situation," Raiden smiled. "I would hate to think you were barreling in without any thought."

"Says the man who is here in Miami instead of in Virginia for a woman that he's never even really talked to. Talk about the pot calling the kettle black," Nic grinned.

Raiden raised his coffee mug in salute, and Nic laughed.

IT WAS DÉJÀ VU all over again.

"I thought you would be gone by now," her mother was saying.

"You thought wrong," Nic responded.

"You're really not needed here," Enid Ross' said in her most supercilious tone. Camilla cringed. She'd always hated it when her mother spoke to her like that.

"That's going to be Cami's decision, Mrs. Ross," Nic said calmly.

Time to enter the fray.

"Good morning, you two." She opened her eyes, then winced. The bright sunlight made her head hurt.

"Camilla, you really need to tell this man to leave," her

mother said as she moved close to her bed. Camilla sighed with relief as Nic started lowering the blinds. Now if he could just do something that would stop all the pain in her arm, without giving her drugs that knocked her flat on her ass.

"Camilla, are you listening to me?"

"I'm sorry, what did you say?" she asked her mother.

"I have to leave tonight. Your doctor said you're not going to be good to fly for three more days. By then your father will be back from Mongolia so he can come and fly back with you to Virginia. I'll have arranged a proper day nurse and night nurse to take care of your needs when you arrive at the house."

Her mother was looking at her smartphone, reading through her action items. How often had Camilla felt like an action item on her mother's to-do list when she was growing up?

Too damn often.

"Mother, I told you I wasn't going home with you," Camilla said in a firm and quiet voice. It was the best way to handle her parents. No emotion. Just stand your ground. When her mother tried to run her over, Camilla just kept on marching along as if her mother had never said a thing.

"Camilla, I already told you how it would be." Her mother's blue eyes glittered down at her.

For just a second Camilla allowed herself to look at Nic standing behind her mother. She took some of his strength and used it as her own.

"Yes, Mother, you did tell me. But I'm twenty-four years old. You don't run my life. I'm not moving in with you. Tell Dad not to bother to come, I'll find my own way home."

"Young lady, this is not acceptable," her mother huffed.

That did bring a smile to Camilla's face. She hadn't been

called 'young lady' in that tone of voice in years. The last time had been when she was dating Nic. How appropriate he should be in the room with them now.

"Mother, I'll take care of myself. I have been for years."

She saw the moment her mother decided to take another tack. "Would you really deny me the right to take care of my only child in her time of need?"

Camilla snorted. That was a good one.

"Mother, you weren't going to take care of me; you said you would hire a day and a night nurse," she explained patiently.

"I would have supervised."

"It doesn't matter. I'm not going home with you. I'm fine on my own."

Her mother gave her a once-over, then sniffed. "Fine. But Camilla Ann Ross, when something goes horribly wrong, you cannot blame it on me."

"Thanks for the vote of confidence Mother," she said to her mother's back as she left the room.

She looked Nic up and down. "So are you round two?" she asked.

He grinned at her. "No, ma'am. I'm too scared to fight with you."

"Smart man."

He picked up the jug of water by the bed and poured her a glass. "Want some? All that arguing probably made your throat dry."

It had. She nodded. He came closer and brought the straw to her lips. She took a long nourishing sip then sighed with satisfaction.

"Do you want more?"

She gave her head a slight shake, anything more would cause her pain.

"Do you need anything else?"

"Do you know when my doctor is making rounds?"

"In two hours, give or take."

"Ohh." She didn't know what else to say.

"Cami, yesterday I asked you to come to my apartment. It's got three bedrooms, one I use as my office, the guest room is really nice. I really do have plenty of leave. Taking care of you would mean the world to me. Did you consider it?"

Cami blushed as she remembered her dream. He was smiling down at her; it was a killer smile as he tried to convince her to do as he asked. Oh, he was laying it on thick. And not like the old days thick, this was a new and improved Nic.

"My mom lives close by," he went on. "I've already talked to her about possibly coming over. She was horrified to hear what happened to you, and she immediately volunteered to come over every day and assist you."

"Absolutely not, I would want to hire a nurse to come in."

His smile was blinding, and she cringed. She realized what she'd said. She'd admitted to actually considering his proposal. Was she out of her mind?

"Whatever would make you feel most comfortable, honey."

"And sit back down, I don't need you hovering over me."

He sat. "Is that better?"

She rolled her eyes. Camilla realized that in all the time her mother had been in the room she had hurt, but now that it was only Nic, her pain had receded quite a bit.

"Nic, be serious for a minute. I need to understand why you would want to take your vacation and babysit me. What are you trying to accomplish?" When she bit her lip it hurt like hell.

"Honey, don't do that, your whole face is bruised, including your lip."

She imagined her face covered with bruises. Her jaw. Her nose. Her mouth.

She jerked back against the pillows as flashes of fists hitting her assailed her. She shook her head, trying to get away. Then she moaned as she remembered hands squeezing her breasts, pinching her nipples. Camilla tried to throw up her hands to protect herself, but they were immobilized. Someone was holding her down. She cried out in pain as her neck and arm burst on fire.

Hands held her head still, the pain in her neck started to stop, but she cried out, hating having someone touch her.

"—Shhh, it's okay. I'm not going to hurt you. You're safe. I'm not going to hurt you. You're safe."

She felt a featherlight touch at her temples going in circles.

"You're safe, Cami. You're in the hospital. Nobody's going to hurt you."

Cami, he called me Cami. It's Nic.

She took in a deep shuddering breath and opened her eyes. Nic looked shattered, his eyes were filled with tears.

"Nic?"

"I'm here, baby. I've got you. You're safe. I promise you."

Camilla shuddered and tried to push back the memories of the men who had hurt her. It wasn't working.

"Please hold me. Hold me, please," she begged. She needed good touches. Loving touches.

"Are you sure?"

"I need you," Camilla whispered.

He curled his arms around her head, his temple next to

hers, their tears mingling. His thumb stroked her cheek with the lightest touch imaginable.

Camilla's arms ached to touch him, absolutely *ached*.

"I'm here, Cami. I'm always going to be here," he whispered against her temple. "You're safe now."

His words were like liquid oxygen; she soaked them in and they gave her life. Over and over again he soothed her with his words, with his touch.

20

"I'm good now," she whispered.

I'm sure as hell not.

Nic lifted his head and looked down at her blue eyes. They were no longer filled with tears. He tried to determine if she was doing better or just saying that to make *him* feel better.

"Truly, Nic, I'm better now."

Her smile was wobbly, but he'd let it go for the moment. He looked her over—not just her face, but her bandaged arms resting over the blankets and her poor bruised face. He knew for a fact that underneath the hospital gown she was covered in bruises all over her chest. It would be a miracle if she were truly 'good'.

"Nic, stop that," she said.

He looked back up and saw her eyes flashing.

"Was that your professor voice?"

"Yes, it was. Did it work?"

He gave her a slow smile. "It's hot."

"You did not just say that." Her eyes were alight with laughter. He couldn't have asked for anything better.

"How often do you lecture? I bet none of the boys ever pass one of your classes, they're too busy fantasizing about you," he teased her, wanting to continue to lighten the mood.

"You are out of your mind." He loved it when she laughed. It was going to be a hell of a long haul to get over the trauma of her kidnapping; laughter was good.

"Seriously though, how are you feeling. How's your pain level?"

She cocked her head to the side and gave him a considering look. "It's manageable. If I have a problem, I'll press the call button for the nurse."

He nodded. "Sounds good." He sat back down and dropped his clasped hands between his knees and tried to pull his thoughts together.

"A little while ago you asked me what I was trying to accomplish having you come and stay with me, right?"

"Right."

He cleared his throat. "I want a second chance."

Once again her blue eyes studied him like they could see right through him. She didn't say anything for the longest time. "I've been thinking about those letters," she started.

"Don't," he said fiercely. "What happened to those letters is in the past. I want to concentrate on our future." He was pretty damn sure he knew what in the fuck happened to those goddamn letters and who he had to thank for them not getting to Cami, but he was serious, that was in the past. What mattered now was going forward.

"All right," she said slowly. "You want to move forward. I get that. Let me get well, then we can date."

"Fuck that noise."

Her eyes went wide. "I beg your pardon?"

Nic shoved himself up off the chair and paced to the

door and back. He clasped the back of his neck with both hands and looked down at Cami. "Sorry, didn't mean to pop off like that." He sucked in a deep breath. "Sure, under normal circumstances I would love to date you, honey. But these aren't normal circumstances. You've been through hell; there is no way you should be alone right now. And I want to be there for you. If you really want to stay in your apartment, that's fine, let me stay with you."

"My apartment is close to the University, so it's really small, it only has one bedroom."

"It's okay, I'll sleep on the couch," he said immediately.

He saw her wiggle her fingers. He reached out and touched them. "Staying at my place is stupid."

Nic had learned how to be patient over the years, so he waited for her to continue.

"Are you sure you want to do this? Really, really sure?"

"Cami, this is our chance. We were too young before, and then later circumstances took away our choices, but fate or God slammed us back together. We were meant to be in this moment, here and now. It's our shot. I don't want to waste it."

Camilla looked up at him and swallowed. "Nic, I want to say something important. Will you listen to me?"

"Always."

"You keep saying you love me, and I have needed to hear that more than you can imagine. But truthfully, you don't know me anymore. I've changed a lot between eighteen and twenty-four; there is no way you can love the me I am today."

Nic hid his smile. He had to be careful and treat her words respectfully, but that was a load of horseshit. He knew this woman down to her bones, this brave, beautiful woman who endured and thrived. He knew Cami Ross down to her toes, and he intended to marry her. But she was right, she needed to be courted. So he was damn well going to get her to stay with him. He'd bring her breakfast in bed every day with a flower on the damn tray. He'd court the hell out of her.

"Nic, tell me what you're thinking," she prompted.

"Huh? Oh, well you're right, honey. We've both changed. Like I said, I want a second chance. I think having you come and stay with me is the perfect way to get to know one another again. Yeah, you could rest and recuperate in your apartment, then we could date for a year. But my way is better. We will know in six weeks if we really have a shot at this."

She bit her lip again and gasped.

"You're going to have to stop doing that."

Her lip went up on the side. "Yeah, I am."

"So do we have a deal? Are you going to let me take care of you?"

"Yes, Nic, we have a deal."

CAMILLA THANKED God that Nic's apartment was on the first floor, she honestly didn't think she could walk up a set of stairs.

She could feel him staring at her as she walked over the threshold of his apartment.

"I'm fine," she said for the ninety-ninth time.

"The sofa is right here, let's get you settled."

It was the only thing she could see in the living room; it had her entire focus. Just about six steps and she'd make it. How could she be trembling so badly? Nic's steady hand was under her left elbow as he helped ease her down.

Camilla closed her eyes with relief when she was finally sitting again, even though it had been only ten minutes since she had been in Kane and A.J.'s sedan.

"It was nice of your friends to pick us up from the airport," she murmured.

"Honey, just sit back and rest, today was a lot. Do you want to go straight to your room? Maybe go to bed for the night or take a nap?"

Camilla's eyes snapped open. "No. I slept on the plane the entire flight, I can't possibly be tired."

Nic chuckled. "No, you're not tired at all," he said facetiously.

"You know what I mean," she tried to snap, but her yawn ruined it.

"How about if I get you something good to eat, not like that box of food we had to pay for on the plane. Would you like that?"

Camilla adjusted her sling. Keeping her injured arm in the exact right position really helped to alleviate unnecessary pain. She massaged her sternum. Now if there was just something to stop her chest from aching as her bruises healed.

"Do I need to bring you a pain pill with food?"

"What kind of food?"

Nic pulled pillows from the other side of the sofa and put them behind her back and gave her one for her lap. It was perfect. "Thanks. So what kind of food?"

"I don't know. I have to check the fridge. Mom said she was going to leave something. That means there are probably enough meals for an entire week."

She could believe it. She remembered the food that was always available at the Hale house when she would go over.

It had seemed like it was Mrs. Hale's life mission to make her gain weight back in the day.

While Nic went to go check the fridge, Camilla leaned back and took a look around her. She was actually kind of shocked; his place was really nice. Like *nice*, nice. If she had to admit, it was put together better than hers. The living room was painted mint green, and there were big black and white photos of forests. Then on another wall was a big grouping of people. Camilla struggled to get up, she wanted a closer look.

"Hey, what are you doing?"

"I wanted to see who everybody was over there," she pointed with her left hand at the pictures on her wall.

"I'll introduce you to everybody later." Nic grinned. "First you're going to eat. You get to choose from chicken and rice or lasagna."

She pursed her lips and raised an eyebrow. "Really? You even have to ask?"

He let out a big laugh. "Hey, you're the one who said I don't know you anymore, I didn't want to assume anything."

"When it comes to Italian food, you are free to assume." She grinned.

"Okay, lasagna it is. Let me put it in the oven. It wasn't in the freezer, just in the refrigerator, so it shouldn't take too long. In the meantime, how about I get you a fruit smoothie?"

She thought about it. "Nah, that'll be too much. Thanks though."

"Be back in a moment. You stay on the couch. Promise?"

She nodded, then watched him walk to the kitchen. God, he looked good from behind. Those jeans really showed off his butt. Camilla took a deep breath.

Down girl, you've just been celibate too long. That's all. After all this time, anybody would be looking good.

She choked back a laugh. *Really? Really? You're going to tell yourself that big of a lie? Soon you'll be saying that bigfoot is real.* She leaned back against the pillows and waited for Nic to return and hoped she could pull herself together before he did.

Once again, the same phrase swirled in her head. "I want a second chance."

She couldn't get those words out of her brain, out of her heart. Was a second chance possible? They weren't those two high school sweethearts anymore who had only eyes for one another. Now they were grown adults with varied experiences and disparate lives of their own. They were just so different. What happened if they did fall in love again; could they make things work?

She sat up straighter and thought about him cradling her head in the hospital, his tears mingling with hers.

Possibly fall in love? What a crock, I'm damn near at the bottom of the love hill.

"Hey, are you out here thinking deep thoughts?"

He held out a bottle of water and she took it gratefully. He'd already taken the top off for her. He sat down beside her on the couch.

"Are those photos by Ansel Adams?" she asked, trying to focus on something tangible.

He looked over his shoulder at the photo over the couch and smiled. "Yeah. We took a couple of family vacations to Yosemite, and I loved it out there. When I saw his photo of Half Dome, I was hooked. I knew I wanted some of his prints in my home."

"So you decorated this place?" she asked tentatively.

He laughed. "What, you thought I had mom do this?"

"Not really, I was thinking a girlfriend," she admitted.

He scooched over on the couch, took the bottle of water out of her hand, and set it down on the coffee table. "There's never been a girlfriend. Don't get me wrong; there have been women, but there's never been a girlfriend."

"Never? Is it because you're gone so much, on those kinds of missions and stuff?"

He gave her a crooked smile. "You met A.J. today. Kane's one of my teammates, she's his wife. So relationships are definitely doable. It just hasn't happened for me. How about you, since I know that you were never engaged to Harris. Anyone serious?"

"There was someone in graduate school," she admitted slowly. "But we both knew it wasn't going to go anywhere."

He frowned. "Why not? Hell, Cami, was he stupid?"

A sense of warmth unfurled in her chest at his words. "He was the furthest thing from stupid as possible. He was going to go teach at Cambridge. He had his path set in stone. His plan was to have a wife who would further his career by hosting dinner parties and making small talk."

"What in the hell did you see in a guy like him?"

She bit her lip. This time it didn't hurt quite as much, but he still noticed. He reached out and slowly touched her face, his thumb gently tugging her lip away from her teeth. "Tell me."

"I guess I was lonely."

"I get that," he said softly. "I've been lonely too."

"Even with..." she waved her hand. "Even with the women?"

He sighed. "Yeah, even with the women. There was never any real connection."

"I'm sorry." And she was.

He took the bottle out of her hand and put it on the

coffee table, took her hand and laced their fingers together. "I'm not. I'm not going to lie and say I've been waiting for you, because I haven't. After I thought you rejected me years ago, I worked hard to put you behind me. But as soon as I heard your name two weeks ago? Hell, Cami, you were all I could think about. The past came flooding back. I realized why my life had been in stasis. I had to get to you."

"I tried to put you behind me too," she admitted. "After all, we were in high school, that kind of relationship never matters, right?"

He gently cupped her cheek. "Wrong. So, so wrong. Looking back, you were the most important person in my life, ever."

Those words hit her right in her heart.

"I'm glad I'm here," she whispered.

"So am I, baby. So am I."

21

THREE DAYS LATER, NIC LOOKED OVER AT CAMI SITTING ON the little patio off the side of his living room. The bruises on her face were clearing up, but that was about all that was getting better. As a matter of fact, things were getting worse.

The first night she'd slept through just fine, but the last two nights she'd had terrible nightmares. Something needed to be done because she was talking less and less. She was closing in on herself. He needed to help her, but he didn't know how.

He went into the kitchen, far enough away that he was positive she wouldn't be able to hear him but close enough that he would still be able to watch her. He called Raiden— he figured as the team medic he could give him some advice.

"Yeah?"

That didn't sound good.

"Hey, Raiden, how are you doing?"

"I'm fine," he answered slowly. "How are you and Camilla?"

"Not so good. She's walling herself up and having

terrible nightmares. She needs counseling, but every time I broach the subject, she just freezes up."

He heard Raiden sigh. "Sounds familiar."

"You're back here in Virginia, right?"

"Yeah. Lisa's old boss from Wilderness Trekkers finally showed up in Miami and flew back with her to Arizona, so I flew home."

Nic didn't respond. What could he say? Raiden's attachment to Lisa didn't really make sense, but when did shit really need to make sense?

"You okay?" Nic finally asked.

"Yeah, I'm fine. Let's focus on Camilla."

"Thanks, man. I suggested counseling, but she shut me down hard. Mom made a brief attempt, but it was too much like me saying something. She crashed and burned."

"You know who might be able to get through to her, is Carys."

"Carys?"

"Yep."

Nic thought about Cullen's wife and tried to think why she could help. Granted, she was a doctor, but still.

"Think about her work with all those abused women here and abroad," Raiden said. "I've talked to Cullen about her, and she's magic. I think you should invite her over, and then get the hell out of there."

"Ya think?"

"Yeah, I really do."

Nic took another look at Cami's still form in the patio chair. She was breaking his heart. "Okay, I'll call Cullen."

"You do that, you won't regret it."

WHEN SHE HEARD the knock on her bedroom door, Camilla looked up from her new phone. She looked back down and realized she didn't even know what book she'd supposedly been reading. She sighed.

"Come in, Nic."

The door slowly opened. He was smiling his Nic smile and she did her best to return it. By the look on his face, she knew she'd failed.

"Cullen's here for a visit. He brought his wife. I ordered some pizza. I made sure there were extra olives. You interested?"

It took her a moment, then she remembered Cullen as the man who had covered her with the cloth back in the jungle. She felt her eyes tingle. She forced back the tears; she was so sick of crying.

"Cami?"

"How can I resist extra olives? I'll be right out."

He shut the door behind him and she took a deep breath. She looked over at the bottle of pain pills and thought about taking one. Her shoulder was only throbbing a little because she'd taken a pill an hour ago so she didn't need one, but it would take the edge off of eating with Cullen and his wife.

She picked up the open bottle with her left hand and stared at it. She really wanted to do it. *Great, add drug addiction to all your other problems.*

She looked at how many pills there were. She had plenty. There was another refill on the bottle.

Fuck that noise!

She snorted out a laugh, surprising herself. God, she really liked that phrase.

I wonder how many other good phrases Nic could teach me.

She put down the bottle, got out of bed, and looked at

her face in the mirror. Okay, pale with dark circles under her eyes. Par for the course. The least she could do was brush her hair. So she did.

When she got out to the living area, she saw that pizza was set up on the dining room table. Nic and the other man stood up.

"You don't have to stand," she insisted.

"My mom would blister my butt if I didn't stand when a lady entered the room," the man she assumed was Cullen answered.

Camilla gave him a wan grin. He held out his hand. "You probably don't remember me, but I'm Cullen Lyons, and this beautiful woman is my wife, Doctor Carys Lyons."

The blonde woman smiled up at her. "Hello, Doctor Ross, it's great to meet you. Nic has been telling us all about you."

Camilla blanched, and Carys must have noticed. "He mentioned that you were a mathematics professor at William and Mary. That's pretty impressive."

Camilla snuck a glance at Nic who was filling up a fourth plate for her. "Why don't you take a seat?" He motioned to a chair that he had already pulled out for her. Camilla sat down across from Carys.

"So you're a doctor, what field do you practice?" Camilla asked.

"I'm taking it easy these days. I do some consulting at two of the hospitals in Virginia Beach."

Carys stood up and reached for a piece of cheesy garlic bread.

"Honey, I would have got that for you," Cullen admonished.

Camilla took note of the gentle curve of Carys' stomach. She guessed that she was about five months pregnant.

"There will come a day when I can't reach across the table. When that happens I'll let you wait on me; until then I'm getting my own food," Carys smiled at her husband.

"Would you like something besides water?" Nic asked Camilla. "There's soda, lemonade, wine?"

"How about lemonade?"

He got up and got her glass of lemonade from the kitchen.

About halfway through dinner, Camilla could actually feel herself come out of her funk a little bit. Cullen was really funny, and Carys was like some kind of nurturing earth mother. She was going to be a fantastic mom.

"So Cullen and I are going to head over to the gym. We're meeting some guys for a basketball game. Will you two be okay alone?" Nic asked.

"Sure," Camilla smiled.

"Is there dessert?" Carys asked.

Cullen laughed. "There's my girl. Nic ordered one of those brownie pies, so you're covered."

Carys blushed and looked over at Camilla. "I can't believe how much I'm eating these days. As a doctor, I know this is part of the process, but as a typical woman I'm thinking it is out of control."

"I can imagine," Camilla said, unsure how to respond.

Nic kissed the top of her head. "Are you sure you're good if we leave? We'll be back in two hours."

She took a deep breath and gave him a reassuring smile, "I'm sure."

"There's my girl," Nic said with a grin. He turned to Carys, "there's milk in the fridge and ice cream in the freezer to go with the pie."

"I'm in heaven."

Cullen went over and gave his wife a lingering kiss. "See

you soon." Camilla looked at the closed door, then looked at Carys, unsure what to say. The guys had already cleared the table, so Carys headed to the kitchen and was soon back out with the brownie pie.

Dammit, I should be helping.

Camilla shook her head, trying to clear her near-constant state of fog. She stood up.

"It's okay, I've got it, you stay where you are. Do you want milk with your brownie?" Carys asked.

Camilla nodded.

Before she knew it, they were sitting across from one another, digging into brownie sundaes. "Who knew a pizza place could make such a delicious dessert, huh?" Carys asked.

"Yeah, who knew."

Camilla appreciated the silence as she ate her dessert, but as it came to an end she started to get curious. "So you and A.J. met your husbands when the teams were on missions?"

"Yep. Did A.J. tell you about the Eurovision Song Contest, and what all went on?" Carys asked.

"She touched on it on the way from the airport, but I was pretty strung out, so it didn't really register. From what Cullen was saying at dinner your time together in Africa was horrifying."

"I wouldn't say that at all." Carys looked at her with a warm expression. "Cullen was just scared for me, Shada, and baby Adam."

"Really?"

"I mean, don't get me wrong, we could have died, but I had faith that Cullen would save us. He's extraordinary. All of those men are."

"Yes. Yes, they are." She pictured Mexico and what

they'd done. Camilla worked mercilessly hard to stop herself from thinking what would have happened if Nic and the others hadn't rescued them.

"Can I ask you a personal question?" Carys' voice was kind and soft.

"You want to know about me and Nic, right?"

"Well if you want to tell me, I would love to hear," Carys replied, her eyes twinkling. "But no, that's not it."

"What then?" Camilla stirred at what was left in her bowl, suddenly not very hungry.

"Well, first I'm going to tell you a little bit more about me. Years ago, I used to be part of Doctors without Borders. I had a horrific experience where I was practically raped. Another SEAL team saved me, but the fallout from that kept me indoors for damn near a month when I got back to the States. Logically I should have known better than that, I'm a physician, I should have known to ask for help, but I didn't. I just shut myself away in my house."

Camilla stared at the woman. How could she talk about it so calmly?

"What did you do?"

"An old family friend came and visited. She saw what was wrong. She made me shower and eat, then she cleaned up the place and called one of my colleagues. Ted ended up dragging me kicking and screaming to a therapist. It was the best thing he could have done. I bless Rosa and Ted every day. They saved me."

"Nic wants me to go see a counselor. His mom suggested it too. I just think time will take care of it." She pushed the dish away from her and melted ice cream sloshed over the side, making a mess on the table.

"Carys, what I don't get is that I was fine while I was in Mexico. I kept it together, you know? I helped others. Why am I such a basket case now? And in front of Nic? I don't want him to see me like this. He says he wants a second chance with me. I think he's serious. Like forever kind of serious, but what if I'm some kind of woman who can't keep it together, who's...who's crying all the time."

She felt tears on her face.

"Let it out," Carys said quietly.

"What if I'm someone who just wants to be in pain so she can take the damn pills so she doesn't have to think or feel? What kind of person am I? Who would want a second chance with that kind of person?" She reached out and snatched up a napkin to sop up her tears.

Camilla didn't know how, but Carys was in a chair beside her, and she was mindfully pulling her into her arms, taking care not to hurt her shoulder.

"Oh honey, I'm so sorry all of this happened to you, I really am. But you were rescued, what, eight days ago?"

"Nine," Camilla said into Carys' shoulder.

"Okay, nine. You've had major surgery, you're still in pain, and from what I understand you've been reunited with the love of your life. I'd say you're entitled to a breakdown, maybe even two or three."

Camilla hiccupped. "You think?"

"I know."

"Carys, I feel so lost. I don't know what to do," she admitted. "I know Nic brought me here to take care of me, but that was because I'm physically injured. I'm sure he wasn't expecting an emotional basket case."

"You'd be surprised. These men understand a hell of a lot more than most. They see things that other men don't see, and it gives them a unique perspective. I'm positive that Nic knew what he was signing up for."

"So I should see one? A therapist I mean. It would actually help me?"

"I hear that you're a genius. Nic's been bragging about you. So I know that you know you should see one. Or at least the normal Doctor Ross would know."

Camilla lifted her head from Carys' shoulder. "That's a lot of 'knows'. You know?"

Carys giggled. "Hey, the woman has a sense of humor, all is not lost."

22

Nic was sitting in the waiting room for Camilla to come out. It was her sixth session with Doctor Cricket in two weeks. He wasn't really surprised that she was going at it so fast. When Camilla made up her mind about something, there was no stopping her. He just wished that she hadn't put a hold on talking about them. She kept insisting that she needed to get her feet back under her before she could contemplate any kind of relationship talk.

The only thing that had Nic keeping it together was that when Camilla had a nightmare, and he went to her in the middle of the night, she held on to him tight. Those nights he would kiss her temple and tell her she was safe, all the time stroking her back. The first night it happened, after she had quieted down, he had eased her back under the covers and attempted to leave. She'd begged him to stay. How could he resist?

They'd developed a pattern. Almost every third night, she would have a nightmare, and he would go to her. Those were the only nights that he could get a good night's sleep.

The office door opened, and Camilla came out, her

smile was blinding. Nic shoved to his feet. He didn't know what in the hell had happened in that room, but he was pretty damned happy about it.

"Do you want to go for lunch?" Camilla asked.

"I don't know, are you buying?" Nic teased.

"Absolutely. Name the place."

"We're definitely going to eat near the water. Let's go."

As soon as they got into his truck, he had to ask her. "So what's got you so excited?"

She blew out a breath and her smile dimmed. "Doctor Cricket made me see something from a different angle. I'd been holding onto a lot of shame—"

"Shame! What in the hell would you have anything to feel shameful about?"

"Nic, just drive the car, would you?"

"Truck, baby. It's a truck."

"Whatever, just drive it."

He knew he was coming on too strong and he needed to dial it back. He gave her a sideways look. "I don't think you appreciate how important a man's truck is to his self-image."

"Maybe you're the one who needs to see Doctor Cricket," she giggled.

Giggling was good. It was *very* good.

"Fish and chips?"

"Oh man, that sounds wonderful. I didn't eat much at breakfast."

"You never do before a counseling appointment," he reminded her. God, it was good to see her looking so good. This reminded him of the bubbly old Cami from high school.

He got them to one of his favorite restaurants in no time, and he wasn't surprised to see Camilla receive some admiring glances from some of the male patrons as they walked to their table. He wanted to put an arm around her waist and let everyone know that she was his, but she still hadn't given him that right and it was eating away at him. He knew she wanted to take things slow, and he needed to respect that, but he *knew* what he wanted.

They both ordered fish and chips and looked out over the water. "So do you want to talk about your session?" Nic asked quietly.

"Not here, but yeah. Let's wait until we get home."

Home. Fuck, he loved that she was calling his place home.

She buttered a roll and took a delicate bite. "But, there *is* something I want to talk to you about."

"Okay."

"Your letters."

Dammit!

He nodded carefully. "Did you want to know what I said in them?"

"I think we've covered that," she whispered, then put her left hand in her lap and looked down. She looked back up at him, tears sparkling on her eyelashes. "I wish I could have read them, I imagine they were beautiful."

"Ah honey, don't cry. Like I said, that's behind us. We're here now. We're going to focus on the future."

"Did you know Mother's been calling? She said that some of her colleagues have been asking about me, and she wants me to come home so she can assure them I'm all right."

What a bitch.

"No, I didn't know she'd been calling." This time he put his hands on his lap so she wouldn't see his clenched fists.

"She did it, didn't she? You said you sent the letters the summer after my junior year of college. You sent them to their house because you knew I'd be there, right?"

He clenched his jaw and nodded.

"I don't think Dad did it; that would have required action on his part, but he would have agreed with mother's decision to send them back to you."

Camilla was sitting up ramrod straight, her eyes boring into his, daring him to disagree with her. "But you've known this for a while, right?"

He nodded again. What else could he say?

"When? When did you guess?"

"Pretty much when you told me you didn't get the letters," he admitted.

This time it was her turn to nod. It was so regal. "You would have let me think you were a liar before throwing the blame on my parents, wouldn't you?"

He rubbed the back of his neck. "Ah hell, I don't know. Pretty quick you said you knew I wasn't a liar, so it was a moot point."

"Here's your food."

He and Camilla looked up and thanked the waitress for their lunch. After she walked away, they didn't give their plates a second glance; instead, they continued to look at one another.

Nic reached out. "Give me your hand Cami."

When she put her hand in his, he laced their fingers together. "What can I do to help?" he asked.

"I don't know. This isn't something for Doctor Cricket. I don't want to get into mommy issues with her. I've been coping with them for fucking years. Up 'til now, I thought I was through the worst of it, but leave it to her to go lower." Her laugh was bitter.

"You can share my mom if you want. She already adores you."

"Thanks," Camilla said softly. Then she sighed and he

watched as she gathered herself up and somehow produced a smile.

"Hey, you don't have to fake a smile for me," he admonished.

She squeezed his hand. "I'm not. I promise. This has been something I needed to talk to you about, and I'm so glad it's out in the open, so I'm happier now, truly."

Nic looked deeply into her blue eyes and saw that she really was smiling.

"You amaze me, Cami."

Her smile got bigger. "In that case, let's eat before the food gets cold."

He nodded.

HER SHOULDER WAS REALLY HURTING, but there wasn't a chance in hell she was going to take a pill before having this next talk with Nic. She could tell he was bracing for something big, and she wanted to be able to explain things correctly, which was going to be tough since she would basically be explaining a bunch of illogical emotions.

"Honey, are you planning to rip the stuffing out of that pillow?"

Camilla looked down and saw that she had actually picked at one of the threads on Nic's sofa pillows and was now plucking at the stuffing. She thrust it away from her.

"I'm so sorry," she exclaimed.

"Forget about it," he said as he sat down next to her. He took her left hand in both of his. "We can talk about anything. Absolutely anything. You know that, right?"

She took a deep shuddering breath. "Yeah, yeah I do. But

you're going to be mad at this one." For a second she gave him a smile. "Mad at me," she clarified. "Not my mother."

"Ah, you caught that, did you?"

"I might have caught on that my mother is not one of your favorite people, yeah."

He rubbed her cold hand. "You're stalling."

"I know." She blew out a deep breath, then looked him in the eye. "This is going to seem so warped, so don't be mad at me, okay?"

"I promise not to be mad at you no matter what, okay honey?"

"Okay. Oh yeah, and don't interrupt me. Can you do that?"

He leaned over and brushed a kiss against her temple. "You look like you're going to shatter apart, Cami. Can I ask *you* a favor?"

She stared at him for a moment, then finally nodded.

"Can I hold you in my arms while you tell me?"

That sounded like heaven. "But how would that work, with my shoulder and everything?"

"Is that a yes?"

She nodded.

"Okay, leave the logistics to me, baby."

He let go of her hand and stood up. Then he gently lifted her into his arms and went over to the big, winged-back chair near the fireplace and sat down, settling her softly onto his lap. He was careful to keep her left side close to his chest. She looked up at him in wonder.

"This feels really nice."

"Yes it does, baby."

She took a few minutes to snuggle closer until she was finally settled in a way that she liked. He felt so good, and she felt safe. Okay, she could do this. She looked at the front of his chest since she couldn't meet his eyes.

"I know you guys were out in the jungle when that man cut off my shirt and was...was..." her breath started coming out faster.

"Slow down honey. Take a deep breath."

"Did you?" she asked. Her left hand clutched at his t-shirt. "Did you?" she asked again.

"Did I what, honey?"

"Did you? Were you?" She looked up at him finally, her face white. "Did you see what happened to me?"

Now it was Nic's turn to take a deep breath. "Yes, I did. I wish I could have saved you from those minutes in that animal's hands, but I couldn't," he bit out. He looked so anguished.

Her shuddering stopped as she gave him a sharp look. "What are you talking about? Your team saved me."

"You spent at least four long minutes under that fucker's hands. I counted every second, Cami. Four long minutes where I couldn't take the shot."

"Take the shot? But wouldn't that have ruined everything if you had? Didn't you all have to be quiet and do a surprise kind of thing?"

He nodded.

"So even though it was supposed to be a surprise, your team still risked the whole mission to save me and Lisa."

"Of course we did! We just had to do it quietly. And I'll regret that to my dying day."

"Oh Nic, maybe my thing isn't so bad now. When I tell you, maybe we can let go of our regrets, our shames, together."

"Again, baby, what do you have to feel ashamed about?

You have never, *ever* done anything wrong in your entire life."

"Here's the part where I don't want you to interrupt, okay?"

"You have my word."

HE SO WANTED to just kiss her and hold her and keep her safe forever, but if all she wanted was for him to listen without interrupting, of course, he could do that.

"All the time we were kidnapped, I kept thinking these kids were my responsibility. I was the teacher, I needed to do something—anything—to take care of them, to keep them safe. I tried so hard to protect them, even when they irritated me, I promise you I did." Her voice started to wobble. "Like when we would have to do our business, our bathroom business in the jungle, Lisa and I would try to make it so the guards couldn't see the girls."

What about you? Who protected and guarded you?

"Sometimes they would make grabs at us, and I'd try to stop them. I'd put myself in between the younger girls, you know?" She looked up at him pleadingly, and he nodded. He could so see her doing just that, but how much abuse did she end up heaping on herself?

"But the night we were tied up in front of the church, El Jefe said we were supposed to be left alone, just guarded." She gave a harsh laugh. "Yeah, like *that* happened. I heard Lisa cry out at the other end of the row. She was in pain. I heard men's laughter. I was frantic to try to help her. So me with my genius brain, I called out. I figured I could get them away from Lisa if I caused a ruckus, right? She'd be safe. What part of figuring out one woman for each man could the genius not have figured out? How could I have been so stupid? Or was I? Maybe I was just wanting that attention. Maybe I was jealous of Lisa."

What the holy fuck, fuck. Was she out of her ever-loving mind?!

She must have seen him ready to interrupt because she slapped her left hand over his mouth. "Don't say anything, okay? Just don't. I don't know how I managed to get my head so mixed up, Nic. I really don't. And I didn't think that way at first. These thoughts started to creep up on me like some kind of jungle vine after I was here for a few days. I was even thinking how it was my fault that Michael Lyton died. He called out for my help when he got El Jefe's rifle after the crash. Everything with the pain from my shoulder and the pain meds just kept getting more and more muddled. I was spiraling. You know?"

"Can I talk now?"

She nodded.

"No I don't understand this, not really," he admitted.

"Really? You don't spiral when you think that you should have been able to save me?"

He thought about what she just said. How many times did he relive those moments when he had that fucking rapist bastard in his scope, and desperately wanted to take a shot. How many times did vomit fill his mouth as he thought about Cami being nude from the waist up, being violated while he did nothing? Hell yes, it was a spiral into hell.

He bowed his head until his forehead was touching hers. "So you really *are* a genius, huh?"

"Yep."

"So how did Doctor Cricket stop you from spiraling? What was today's breakthrough?"

"Like I said, she made me think of it from a different angle."

Nic couldn't wait. He didn't give a shit if the breakthrough helped him, all that mattered was that it had helped Cami. "Tell me."

"All she did was ask me if I thought the others brought it on themselves. I practically yelled out the word, '*No.*' I was appalled at her even thinking that. They were victims."

Nic nodded. "Of course they were. Victims of animals."

"Exactly right," Camilla agreed vehemently. "Then she asked me what made me think I was somehow different than any of them. What set me apart? Who made me God?"

Nic felt a smile forming. The doctor was good. Really good.

"What did you say to that?"

"Well, I blustered for a while, saying how I was the teacher, and I was in charge, and that made me different from the rest. Then she gave me the gotcha question."

Now Camilla grinned. Her eyes actually sparkled.

Nic was seeing where this was going but he still asked. "What was the gotcha question?"

"She wanted to know if that meant that Lisa, who was the tour guide, had brought this on herself."

"Once again I practically yelled, '*hell no.*' All Doctor Cricket had to do after that was raise her eyebrow. I got it. I really got it. All that shame I'd been holding melted away. Nic, it just melted away. Can you believe it?"

"Yes, baby, I can."

She reached up and stroked his cheek. "So you see how you can't blame yourself?"

He thought about lying but that wasn't who they were. "Not really."

"How many of your team members were dying to stop what was happening to Lisa and me?"

He didn't answer.

He felt her finger trace the cleft in his chin. "Honey? Can you answer me?"

"Every single one of us who could see what was happening," he admitted.

"Do you blame them for not taking a shot, or do you think they did the right thing to wait?"

With every fiber of his being, he wanted to say it wasn't the same. But looking into those solemn blue eyes, he couldn't. She was right. She was absolutely right.

"Nic?"

"Hmm?"

"Do you think that maybe you can forgive yourself?" she asked quietly, her fingers still caressing his face.

"I think I might be able to start."

"That's all I can ask."

23

"I AM SO SICK OF DOING EVERYTHING LEFT-HANDED," CAMILLA huffed. When Nic laughed, she gave him a side-eyed glare. "That is so not funny."

"Yes, ma'am."

"I am also sick of this apartment. I'm going stir crazy."

"Yes, ma'am."

"If you call me ma'am one more time I'm going to hit you!"

Nic seriously considered calling her ma'am again to see what would happen, but he refrained. He also didn't point out that they had just been to her apartment three days ago to pick up a suitcase worth of clothes and toiletries, and spent the night there. He at least had the good sense not to try to use logic at this point, not when she was so riled up.

"Is it okay if I tell you you're beautiful when you're angry?"

Camilla marched to the sofa, picked up one of the decorative pillows, and threw it at him. He let it hit him, figuring that would give her a little bit of satisfaction. Anyway, he had been telling the truth; she was wearing an orange sundress that looked fantastic with her pale skin and chestnut hair.

"Stop smiling." Her eyes narrowed and she picked up another pillow.

Oh no, he wasn't having that.

He strode toward her.

"Don't you dare come near me, Nicholas Hale. I'm armed and dangerous." She lifted the pillow high over her head. Nic easily took it out of her hand and tossed it back onto the sofa. He wrapped his arm around her waist and pulled her close.

"It seems to me that you have a lot of excess energy today. Maybe we need to find a way for you to channel it."

"I don't know what you're talking about," she huffed.

Things had been coming to a head since her breakthrough four days ago. "How is your shoulder?" he asked. "Are you in pain?"

"No," she whispered. She looked up at him, her eyes dark with desire. Oh yeah, it was time. Nic's breathing stopped as he contemplated her full lips and flushed face. Years, it had been years since he had kissed her. Her left arm snaked around his neck and she tried to pull his head down, breaking him out of his trance.

Go easy. You need to take it easy, man.

Nic tilted his head and slanted his lips over hers. Memories burst into his brain, immediately overpowered by the sublime beauty of *this* moment. Camilla's mouth flowered open, welcoming a deeper kiss as she pulled him even tighter. His eyes started to drift shut but he slammed them open, wanting to watch the woman in his arms, not wanting to miss anything about their new first kiss.

He slid his tongue into her mouth and she moaned. He was lost in the pleasure of her heat and taste. Over and over again, he kissed and nipped at her mouth. She melted against him and he gladly took her weight, as both hands caressed her ass through the thin cotton of her dress. She ground her front against his arousal, rocketing his desire higher and higher.

He had to stop. One more instant and he would be carrying her into his bedroom, and it was too soon. They still had things to work out.

He slowly pulled away from their kiss and looked down at her dazed expression.

"Why did you stop?"

"It's too soon to take this step," he whispered. "Please know that I want to make love to you, but I want to make sure we do this at the right time."

Her brow furrowed. "What are you talking about?"

He moved one hand and stroked her back in long sweeps. "Our relationship talk. You said you wanted to wait until you got your feet back on the ground, remember?"

Camilla stepped back and Nic loosened his hold. "Honey, despite what I said back then, we've been moving forward all along. At least that's how it's seemed to me. Am I wrong?" Camilla asked.

"Oh hell no. I've been getting to know you for the last four weeks. The new and improved Cami, and I've been impressed as hell."

He watched her blush. How could she be blushing?

"Well don't be too impressed, I'm pretty boring. I've been at the same University for six years," she reminded him.

"Yeah, and how many papers have you written? What about the time you were asked to teach a semester in Ireland? I would say that was pretty impressive."

"That's boring math stuff," she protested. "You're out saving lives."

"I thought I was just a glorified thug that Uncle Sam pays to do their dirty work," he teased.

"Never say that!" Camilla said in a horrified voice. "Don't you dare."

Nic laughed.

"I'm serious, Nic, don't even say that in jest."

He held up his hands. "Okay, I promise."

"As for our relationship building, I've been getting to know you too. You're one amazing man. Watching you cook blackberry cobbler and then taking it over to Mimi and Alice was a great day. I learned a lot about you."

Nic flushed. He'd been worried when he'd left Alice and Camilla alone while he'd played with Mimi in the backyard. "What do you mean you learned a lot about me?"

"There's too much to go into," she waved her hand then she rested it on his chest. "You have such a good heart, Nic."

"I see a man who found a way to get me into counseling when I needed it. A man who sees to my physical needs when I'm in pain. A man who cares deeply for his cousin and her child. Your generosity of spirit overwhelms me."

Nic held her gaze even though it was hard under all that praise. "I love how we play together too. I love how you're smarter than me."

Nic snorted, "how in the hell am I smarter than a genius?"

"You see things about people that I miss. Even small things like that waitress at the restaurant. You knew to ask her about her baby because you saw a little bit of spit-up on her shoulder. You got her talking and smiling when she was clearly dead on her feet."

"It's part of my job to notice things."

"Yeah sure. I'm buying that." Camilla rolled her eyes.

"Anyway, I've definitely gotten to know you, and I'm dazzled by you."

She paused, then cleared her throat.

"Let me be as clear as possible, okay?"

He nodded. Waiting.

"I love you. I love you now and I loved you then. And if I'm totally honest with myself I think I've loved you all the time in between."

He froze, then clasped her hand where it was still resting on his chest.

"I love you more than words can say, Cami. My heart beats because yours does." He couldn't help the rasp in his voice.

She gave him a slow, sultry smile. "Does that mean we can make love now?"

He ran the back of his knuckles down her jaw. "Oh honey, the things I'm going to do to you," he whispered.

Nic bent down and picked her up, enjoying her little squeak of surprise. He was careful of her injured shoulder, already considering how he was going to make love to her without causing her any pain.

He didn't let her down until they were in front of his bed. Then he indulged in another heady kiss, a kiss that only Cami could provide. It was like water in the desert. She slid her hand underneath his t-shirt and he shuddered with pleasure. In the meantime, he worked down the zipper of her dress. The only time he pulled back from the kiss was to help get her arms out of the straps.

"I've got to tell you that there has been a huge upside to your shoulder injury," Nic said as he lowered her dress down past her hips.

"What's that?"

"You never wear a bra."

"I know, even when the nurse was here in the beginning to help me into one I didn't put it on. I can't unhook it at night, so it's easier to go without."

Nic brushed her breasts with the tips of his fingers and her nipples hardened. "I've had hundreds of fantasies of these breasts in the four weeks you've been here."

"Hundreds, huh?"

"Maybe more."

Her nails scraped the length of his chest beneath his t-shirt. "Take this off," she commanded.

"Yes, ma'am."

"Say that again, and I'll give you trouble," she warned.

He pulled the shirt over his head and then grinned down at her. "What kind of trouble?"

"Good trouble."

He felt himself flush as she stared at his chest.

"You've changed. I mean, you were always built, but now you have a man's body, you know?"

Nic chuckled. "Should I take that as a compliment?"

She leaned forward and rubbed her face against his broad chest. "Oh yeah, it's definitely a compliment."

Feeling her bare breasts against his body was the best kind of torture imaginable. Then she was kissing him, her lips soft. Then he felt her teeth scrape over his lips and he thought his head might explode.

He walked her backward until her legs hit the end of the bed. He eased her down to a sitting position. He knelt down in front of her.

"Are you sure you're ready for this?" he asked one last time.

She laughed. "You're a nut if you have to ask that again."

He grinned, and then he gripped her panties and pulled

them off, flinging them over his shoulder. Her eyes went wide when he widened her thighs.

"Are you going to—"

He looked away from her silken folds and met her eyes. "You bet I am."

"That was never on the menu before." She sounded very excited.

"This is the new and improved menu." He coaxed her legs just a little wider. "Lay back."

"No, I want to watch." Yep, she was definitely excited.

His thumbs parted her lower lips and he groaned when he saw how wet she was for him. She was breathing fast and her hand fisted in his short hair. He licked along the seam of her sex and delighted in her moan of excitement. Her taste was unbelievable; clean and tart and all things Cami. He moved upwards and circled his tongue around her clit. She bucked up against him.

"Oh God, Nic."

Her nails bit into his scalp.

He sucked her swollen bundle of nerves into his mouth, then laved it with his tongue. She began to moan in earnest. Nic slowly slid a finger into her tight sheath and Camilla shuddered. Her channel squeezed his digit hard, she was so close. He sucked harder and went a little deeper and she cried out.

"Nic!" she wailed.

He stood up and helped her to the middle of the bed and laid down beside her. Minutes later, her blue eyes shot open. "Is making love on the menu?" she asked.

"Oh yeah."

"Then take off those damn jeans."

24

CAMILLA STRETCHED AND REACHED FOR NIC, BUT HE WASN'T in bed beside her. She looked at the window and squinted; she could see that the sun was pretty bright behind the blinds. Just how late was it?

She sat up, pulling the sheet up over her breasts. When she looked around the room, she saw one of her sleep shirts lying across the bottom of the bed. Could the man be any more thoughtful?

After she put on the shirt, she opened the door and smelled bacon.

"You interested in breakfast?" Nic called out.

Her stomach rumbled with interest.

"Yep. Let me pull on some clothes." She'd shower after breakfast.

She went to the bathroom down the hall and took care of her morning business including brushing her teeth. She tried to tame her hair, but no matter what she did, it still looked like sex hair. A shower and shampoo after breakfast would take care of that. She threw on shorts and a t-shirt and found Nic in the dining room already, with two plates set up.

"You're not expecting me to eat all of this, are you?" Camilla grabbed the big glass of orange juice and started drinking before she even sat down.

"We'll just see. My guess is that you're going to be pretty hungry. I already had a blenderful of smoothie. This is my second breakfast."

"No wonder you go work out every day."

"Yep, this body doesn't happen by accident."

Camilla plopped some of her cheesy scrambled eggs on her toast and took a bite. "This is wonderful. I'm going to have to start working out at this rate."

"You're perfect just the way you are."

He sure as hell made her feel that way last night.

"So, besides my doctor's appointment, what's on today's agenda?"

Nic raised his eyebrow and gave her a slow smile.

How could she go from eating breakfast to hot for his body in less than a second?

"My doctor's appointment is in two and a half hours. I think we have some time to kill, don't you?"

"Finish your breakfast, miss; you're going to need your strength."

Camilla laughed and put another forkful of cheesy eggs onto her toast. When the doorbell rang, Nic went to go answer it and she kept eating. Lately, there had been a lot of salespeople coming through the apartment complex. Nic always answered and politely told them no. He really was a nice guy.

"I want to talk to her," she heard her mother say.

Oh, bloody hell.

Camilla hastily put down her fork and took a swig of her

orange juice, then wiped her mouth with the paper towel. By the time she got up and turned around, her mother was in the middle of the living room. She was all decked out in one of her power pantsuits. She was even wearing her clunky gold choker made of real gold. Yep, she meant business, and Camilla saw red. This was the woman who had sent back Nic's letters.

She gave Camilla a long once over and pursed her lips. "Really, this is how you're dressing now? You look like a freshman at a community college."

"God forbid," Camilla said. Nic winked at her over her mother's shoulder. It helped. Maybe she could do this without screaming like a banshee.

"You haven't answered my calls or texts. You've forced me to come."

"Actually, I didn't Mother. I would have thought you would get the message that I didn't want to talk to you right now. And I don't. I'm pissed off at you, and it's going to take a long time before I can talk to you in a reasonable tone."

Her mother pulled up her purse strap and stood straighter. "Really, Camilla, I don't condone language like that. Clearly, this man has been a bad influence. Get your things, we're leaving now."

"Like hell we are. The only person who's leaving is you."

"Camilla Anne, don't take that tone with me, it's uncouth. I don't want you dragged through the mud. You need to—"

"I've had it—" Nic started.

"Stuff it Nic, this is my fight." Camilla turned back to her mother. "If you think you can waltz right in here and tell me what to do? You're out of your ever-loving mind!"

"Camilla—"

"Shut it, Mother. I've had enough of your shit to last a

lifetime. You did your damndest to ruin my life. I cannot believe that you sent back the letters that Nic sent to the house."

"I did no such thing!" Enid Ross' hand fluttered against her necklace. Camilla was familiar with that tell; she always did that when she was lying.

"I said shut up. I'm talking this time. But for the grace of God, I would have traveled this earth without having the man I love in my life. All because of your elitist venom. I have never, not once, understood what I could have possibly done wrong to not earn your love as a child. But I eventually resigned myself to it. At ten years old I realized that you just didn't have any love to give. Then I started to want your respect, and I tried to mold myself into the perfect little Ph.D., hoping one day I would be good enough for you. But when I wanted one ounce of happiness for myself, when I found someone who *could* love me, you set out to destroy it."

Nic was now at her side. She reached out her hand and he clasped it.

Enid took a steadying breath. "Camilla you're overwrought. Perhaps it's best if I come back at another time. Next week maybe."

"I'm not overwrought. I'm thinking very clearly. If at some time in the future, I want to reestablish a relationship with you, I will let you know."

"Camilla, that's unacceptable. You're my daughter. Of course, we will talk."

Camilla laughed. "For God's sake, Mother, we've never really had a conversation. All that you do is talk *at* me. I'm sick of it, and I won't deal with a woman who tried to destroy my life."

"And your father?"

"Give me a straight answer. Did he know about the letters?"

Enid shifted and her eyes shied away from her.

"Mother, I want an answer, did Dad know?

Enid gave a small nod.

"Then the same thing goes for him."

"We were only doing what we thought was the right thing." She said, her voice devoid of emotion.

"One little, tiny part of me knows that, Mother. That's the only reason I'm saying it is *possible* that I might one day open the door back up. But don't hold your breath."

"I—" Enid started.

"Let me walk you to the door," Nic said as he stepped in front of Camilla.

When she looked at Nic she again looked like she was sucking on a lemon. "I can see myself out." She turned and walked out the door. As soon as she was gone, Nic turned back to Camilla and took her into his arms.

"Are you all right?"

She nodded.

"Words, baby. I need words."

"Nic, I wish I could say I really feel something, some kind of loss, you know? But I would feel worse if I had lost one of my teaching assistants. And I'm not even worrying that there's something wrong with me. I basically said goodbye to my mother, in my heart, years ago. I just did it in real life this time, does that make sense?"

He touched his forehead to hers. "Yes, it does. And your father?"

"I cared about the image of him, but he was never really around. He was always out of the country on some dig or another. But knowing he was complicit in keeping us apart? Nope, I can't do it. He's in time-out with Mother."

Nic chuckled. "You know I'll support you no matter what. If and when you want them back in your life, I'll be able to be civil to them, you know that, right?"

"You're such a nice man. Yeah, I know that."

"But if she's a bitch to you, the gloves come off. There's no picking on my Cami."

"Am I your Cami?" she asked softly.

"Damn right you are. I love you, you can take that to the bank."

EPILOGUE

CAMILLA STRETCHED BEFORE GETTING INTO HER HATCHBACK. Her neck was still tight, but a massage from Nic should clear that up. Of course, the one-hour drive to his place was only going to make it worse. Thank God it was the start of spring break; God knew she needed a vacation. She placed her bulging satchel in the passenger seat and started the car.

As she made her way onto the highway, she thought about her talk with Roxanne in her office that afternoon. It was the girl's first time back on campus. She was considering taking classes next year and she wanted Camilla's advice. Roxanne hadn't been the first of the kidnapped students to come and talk to her, and she was glad. It was good to see that they were all gradually recovering. When she found out that Roxanne hadn't sought counseling, Camilla had advocated hard that she do so. She'd even shared her experience with her therapist. She crossed her fingers that the girl would try it.

She looked over at the briefcase and thought about all the e-mails that were on her computer. It was time to talk seriously to Nic about the career change she wanted to make. She was being headhunted by a couple of companies that were offering her some consulting work that she could do from home with minimal travel. The predictive analysis work that they wanted her to do dovetailed nicely with the papers she had written. She was almost one-hundred percent sure Nic would support her in this decision, but there was still a niggling doubt. If he would just propose, then everything in her world would be great.

That was when she'd decided to take the bull by the horns. For God's sake, she and Nic had even discussed the fact that they wanted a large family because they both grew up as only children. It should be a done deal, and she was sick of waiting. Who said that the man always had to propose anyway? She wanted to get their life together started. She loved this man with every particle of her being, and she knew deep in her heart that he loved her too. She was tired of waiting, she wanted him tied to her. Now.

This coming vacation would be a perfect time to propose.

If you're so confident, why are your hands sweaty? she asked herself in the rearview mirror?

"Shut up. It's going to be fine."

NIC SNAPPED the ring box shut and shoved it into the pocket of his cargo shorts. He loved Camilla desperately and had wanted to marry her for years. But since they'd been back together there was one thing stopping him. He wanted to make sure she could handle it when he just up and left in the middle of the night to go on a mission. He knew that she'd worry and wait. It was a lot to ask of someone. Could she handle it?

Since she'd gone back to teaching, he'd been away three times. He didn't know how, but Camilla had handled it just as well as his other teammates' women. She was incredible. She didn't pester him for details, she just welcomed him home with open arms. He had really watched her to make sure she wasn't putting on a false front, but she wasn't. So it was time. He couldn't wait to make her his wife.

Nic had been up in the air as to where to take Camilla for vacation. He sure as hell wasn't going to take her anywhere tropical. When it turned out that Kane and A.J. were going away for a week and Kane offered up his lake house, Nic jumped at the chance to use it. Camilla was really beginning to relax. He knew that school had really been stressing her out lately.

Tonight he was going to do some grilling and make her a margarita so they could enjoy the sunset out on the deck.

"Do you need any help in there?" Camilla asked as she came into the kitchen.

He looked down at the steaks that he'd marinated and shook his head. "No, I'm good. The potatoes are already on the grill, I'll put these on now." He handed her a strawberry margarita which she gladly accepted. He grabbed a beer for himself.

"Hmmm, this tastes good," she said as she took a sip.

"It'll taste even better with dinner," he promised.

He hustled them outside and soon had them eating a perfectly prepared meal. "You did good, Mister Hale."

"Why thank you, Doctor Ross," he grinned at her. "Would you like another margarita while we sit in the lounge chairs?"

"No, I'm good."

They both went about cleaning up the dishes and putting them in the sink, then came back out to the deck.

232 | CAITLYN O'LEARY

Camilla started sitting down in one of the chairs, but Nic pulled her into his arms and sat her down on his lap.

"Oh, I like this," she said as she snuggled into his warm body. So did Nic. He always liked how Camilla's body fit perfectly into his.

She looked up at him, her eyes shimmering with magic. He could tell she wanted to say something.

"What, love?" he asked.

She struggled with the pocket of her sundress, then pulled out a small white box.

"What's this?"

"Open it, Nic."

He looked into her eyes again. They were a little bit anxious, so he kissed her. Then he opened the box and saw two matching platinum rings, one sized for a man, the other for a woman.

"Will you marry me?" she asked huskily.

Part of him wanted to laugh but he couldn't, he was too moved. He took a deep shuddering breath. He cupped her cheek and gave her a tender, lingering kiss. "It would be my honor to marry you, Cami. There is nothing in this world that would make me happier."

He set the box beside the lounge chair then pulled her closer and kissed her deeper. Finally, they pulled apart. "Since we have to wait until after the wedding to wear them, I have an idea," Nic said.

"Okay." Camilla smiled. She had that dazed look that said they would soon be making love.

Nic pulled out a smaller blue box from his pocket and flipped it open. "Cami, will you marry me?"

She sat up and her eyes got as wide as her smile. "Really? You were going to propose tonight?"

"Really, I was going to propose tonight."

She thrust out her left hand. "Can you put it on me?"

He gently pushed the emerald and diamond ring onto her finger. When he looked up she was laughing and crying.

"I couldn't ask for anything better, Nic. Not anything."

"Growing old with you will be the best thing that ever happens to me," he said as he pulled her in for a long kiss.

For Raiden and Lisa's story, check out "Her Noble Protector"

ABOUT THE AUTHOR

Caitlyn O'Leary is a USA Bestselling Author, #1 Amazon Bestselling Author and a Golden Quill Recipient from Book Viral in 2015. Hampered with a mild form of dyslexia she began memorizing books at an early age until her grandmother, the English teacher, took the time to teach her to read -- then she never stopped. She began re-writing alternate endings for her Trixie Belden books into happily-ever-afters with Trixie's platonic friend Jim. When she was home with pneumonia at twelve, she read the entire set of World Book Encyclopedias -- a little more challenging to end those happily.

Caitlyn loves writing about Alpha males with strong heroines who keep the men on their toes. There is plenty of action, suspense and humor in her books. She is never shy about tackling some of today's tough and relevant issues.

In addition to being an award-winning author of romantic suspense novels, she is a devoted aunt, an avid reader, a former corporate executive for a Fortune 100 company, and totally in love with her husband of soon-to-be twenty years.

She recently moved back home to the Pacific Northwest from Southern California. She is so happy to see the seasons again; rain, rain and more rain. She has a large fan group on Facebook and through her e-mail list. Caitlyn is known for telling her "Caitlyn Factors", where she relates her little and big life's screw-ups. The list is long. She loves hearing and connecting with her fans on a daily basis.

Keep up with Caitlyn O'Leary:

Website: www.caitlynoleary.com
FB Reader Group: http://bit.ly/2NUZVjF
Email: caitlyn@caitlynoleary.com
Newsletter: http://bit.ly/1WIhRup

facebook.com/Caitlyn-OLeary-Author-638771522866740

twitter.com/CaitlynOLearyNA

instagram.com/caitlynoleary_author

amazon.com/author/caitlynoleary

bookbub.com/authors/caitlyn-o-leary

goodreads.com/CaitlynOLeary

pinterest.com/caitlynoleary35

ALSO BY CAITLYN O'LEARY

Her Unbroken Seal (Book #11)

BLACK DAWN SERIES

Her Steadfast Hero (Book #1)

Her Devoted Hero (Book #2)

Her Passionate Hero (Book #3)

Her Wicked Hero (Book #4)

Her Guarded Hero (Book #5)

Her Captivated Hero (Book #6)

Her Honorable Hero (Book #7)

Her Loving Hero (Book #8)

THE FOUND SERIES

Revealed (Book #1)

Forsaken (Book #2)

Healed (Book #3)

SHADOWS ALLIANCE SERIES

Declan

Printed in Great Britain
by Amazon

24429384R00136